*Enjoy this wonderful
Jamaican animal Story
One Love!
Roger Williams*

TURN BACK BLOW

TURN BACK BLOW

Roger Williams

This book is dedicated to all mistreated and abused animals in the world.

ACKNOWLEDGMENT

This book would not be possible without the encouragement of my friends and family. A special thanks to the Almighty God who stood by me throughout the writing process. Many thanks to my cousin Faith and my best friend, Nicholas, for their encouragement. Thanks to my uncle Audley and good friend Maurice Bullock—who took the time out to answer some of my research questions. Thanks to my parents for believing in me, and Ms. Brittany Humes, who proofread the manuscript and gave me her wonderful feedback. Last, but not least, I must thank my fans, who supported me throughout the years.

CHAPTER ONE

It was a hot day in August. Like a fiery ball, the midday sun glowed brightly in the sky. A heavy, warm breeze blew over the town of Iron Bridge, a small community in the parish of Saint Catherine, Jamaica. The warm breeze traveled toward the Rio Cobre River, where Bruck Kitchen, a large, five-year-old, gray-and-black male cat, sat beneath an avocado pear tree by the riverside. Bruck Kitchen finished the last of the ripe avocado pear he had been eating and licked his lips.

"Mmmm," he said to himself, licking both of his front paws. "Is a good thing a come early, else some other puss would a find this good pear on the ground."

The blare of a truck horn disturbed his tranquility. He looked toward the main road that ran just above the river. "Them humans and them noisy vehicles," he murmured. He wiped a smudge of pear residue from his whiskers with a front paw.

The voices of humans caught Bruck Kitchen's attention. He looked in the direction of the sound and saw that it was coming from a small dirt road that led from the main road to the riverside. Three humans were walking down the dirt road. All three were in their early teens. They were two males and one female. One of the human males had a long fishing pole in his hand. The other carried a small box of worms.

Bruck Kitchen chuckled. "A think a was the only one hunting food in this hot sun." He quickly lost interest in the humans and began to search for more of the avocados that usually fell from the tree. He saw the round bottom of one of the green-skinned fruits beneath a calabash tree that had grown close to the avocado tree. The rest of the fruit was covered with dead, dry leaves from the calabash tree. He walked to the fruit while licking his lips.

Suddenly, a frightening scream shattered the afternoon air. Bruck Kitchen made a quick U-turn and dashed up the rough trunk of the avocado tree. He halted on a limb and looked down to see what had caused the scream. Close to the river's edge, he saw the female human pointing at a partially submerged log that was floating in the middle of the muddy-looking water. One of the male humans picked up a stone and threw it at the log. The stone hit the log and bounced in the air before falling into the water. The log started to move toward their side of the riverbank.

Bruck Kitchen realized that it was not a log. "Rahtid, them don't see is a crocodile that!" he said. He climbed farther up the tree and settled on a solid branch. "A not coming out a this tree, you know." He looked down, where he saw a few other humans looking at the crocodile. "A where so much humans come from in a short time?" he whispered. Bruck Kitchen looked around for the female teenager who had seen the crocodile in the water, but she was nowhere on the riverbank. He spotted Lanky Roy, a tall and skinny young man, pointing at the crocodile in the river. Lanky Roy was in his early thirties and was one of the many illegal taxi operators living in the community. He had a slingshot in one of his hands.

"Rahtid, is Lanky Roy that," said Bruck Kitchen, "a hear him hunting mi down. A now mi not coming out a this tree, lightning will have to strike mi up in here." Bruck Kitchen climbed even farther up the avocado pear tree and hid among a bunch of leaves. Through a gap in the leaves, he watched as more humans started to climb down the dirt road that led from the main road. Even a few of the noisy vehicles on the main road had started to slow down. Bruck Kitchen turned his attention back to the crocodile incident taking place at the riverside. The crowd of humans on the riverbank had gotten larger. A few of the humans walked cautiously to the edge of the river to get a closer look at the large crocodile while most of them watched from a distance. Yabba, a local tire repairman who wore his hair in a cornrow style, was one of the humans looking at the crocodile in the river. Yabba was Lanky Roy's best friend and was given the nickname Yabba because he had a large mouth and a pair of lips that looked like two pieces of cow liver. In his hand, Yabba had a long piece of wooden stick with a short piece of rope attached to it. The rope was tied in a noose knot. Yabba walked to the edge of the riverbank and tried to get the noose around the crocodile's head, but he was unsuccessful.

Lanky Roy watched as Yabba tried to noose the crocodile. The tall, lanky man tucked the slingshot that he had in his hand into the waist of his pants and took the stick from Yabba. He tried to get the noose around the uncooperative crocodile's head, but his attempt also failed.

"Yow, Lanky," said Yabba. He signaled with a hand for Lanky Roy to follow him.

Lanky Roy threw down the piece of stick on the muddy riverbank and followed Yabba in the direction of the avocado pear tree.

* * *

Up in the avocado pear tree, Bruck Kitchen watched Lanky Roy and Yabba walk toward the tree and stop at its root. Bruck Kitchen felt like he wanted to disappear into thin air; he held his breath while he trembled and looked down at both male humans. Even though he was safe in the tree, Lanky Roy was too close for his comfort. Earlier that morning, one of his cat friends had told him that Lanky Roy was hunting for him. He thought his friend was joking, but after seeing the slingshot in Lanky Roy's hand, he knew his friend wasn't playing around. Bruck Kitchen's limbs were shaking on the tree limb. He tried to keep still so he could eavesdrop on the conversation below.

Lanky Roy pulled the slingshot from his waist and twirled it around on his right index finger as Yabba started to explain to him in a hushed tone.

"A have a idea," said Yabba, looking around to see if anybody was watching them. "Why you don't use the worthless mongrel dog that you have up a you yard as bait?"

Lanky Roy looked at Yabba as if he didn't understand what Yabba was saying to him. "As bait?"

"Yeah, mon. A believe that the croc would a find a mongrel dog more enticing than a old dry stick and a piece a rope."

"Oh," said Lanky Roy. He was getting more interested in Yabba's idea.

"Yeah, mon, we could tie a long piece a rope around the mongrel neck and throw him to the croc. When the croc grab on him, we just pull in the rope and capture the croc. What you think?" Yabba's eyes sparkled with enthusiasm while he waited for Lanky Roy's opinion on his plan.

Lanky Roy pointed a finger at his friend. "Good idea, Yab. From that mongrel dog allow the police to come in the yard and don't bark, a hate him. A almost end up a prison for thieving electricity to rahtid." He looked around at the crowd watching the crocodile in the river and shook his head. "It cost mi a ton load a money a courthouse."

A few months ago, one of Lanky Roy's friends had shown him how to beat the system and bypass the meter that the electrical power company had installed on his house. The power company had suspected Lanky Roy's low monthly bills and launched an investigation.

"Lanky, when you thieving electricity, you cannot leave you gate open, especially when you have a worthless mongrel dog in a you yard."

Lanky Roy knew that his friend always told him the truth. He seldom admitted to it, but this time he had no choice but to agree that Yabba was right. "A true you talking. Anyway, a long time a want get rid a that mongrel dog, now that a have a Rottweiler, a don't have no use for a mongrel dog again."

"A true, mon." Yabba laughed. "Probly in the next life, the mongrel will learn that when him see police, him must bark and warn him master."

Lanky Roy stepped off. "Real talk, a soon come. A have some rope at the house too." He returned the slingshot to the waist of his pants and ran off in the direction of his house.

*　　*　　*

Up in the avocado tree, Bruck Kitchen shook his head.

"Them two man wicked, eh?" he grumbled to himself. He watched Yabba walk back to the riverside. "Them must be joking, them can't serious. Mi have to see if them really going use the mongrel dog as bait." He covered himself with more leaves while he waited nervously to see what would happen next.

CHAPTER TWO

The Johnson Lane Housing Scheme in the Iron Bridge community was about half of a mile from the river. The housing scheme was built in the late 1980s and was populated by low-income residents. The houses in the scheme were mostly two-bedroom houses made out of concrete and cement blocks, each surrounded by a five-foot concrete wall. The only building that was not made out of concrete and cement blocks was a one-room board building that was at the extreme bottom of the scheme. It belonged to Yabba, who lived in it and used its backyard to repair car tires. The roof of the board building was covered with a few rusty sheets of galvanized zinc. The structure stood out among the rest of the houses like a sore thumb.

Lanky Roy's house was about three houses away from Yabba's board house. Like most houses in Jamaica, Lanky Roy's house had burglar bars. The bars were made from half-inch steel and were painted with white gloss paint. Several diamond-shaped patterns were welded onto them. The bars ran along the veranda of the house, all exterior doors, and covered all windows from the outside.

A white Toyota Corolla station wagon, with several patches of paint missing, was parked outside the gate. Inside the yard, there was an overflowing East Indian mango tree. Dozens of green mangoes hung heavily in bunches of three and four from the tree limbs. A newly constructed wooden doghouse sat beneath the mango tree. A huge black-and-brown Rottweiler with a glistening silver chain around its neck was fast asleep outside the doghouse.

*   *   *

At the back of the house, Clifton, a ten-year-old boy who walked with an awkward limp, sat underneath a large ackee tree, talking to Mongrel, an eight-year-old, male mongrel dog. Mongrel was ash gray in color and had an old piece of rope around his neck for a collar. With an effort to loosen the piece of rope collar, Mongrel tugged at it with a front paw and looked at his human friend. "Clifton, a think you should go start you yard work before Lanky Roy woman come round here and say you a idle."

"Idle, she don't see how the sun hot?" asked Clifton. "Sometime she talk too much."

"Yesterday, she tell the mailman that you crazy because you talk to mi?"

Clifton wasn't surprised that both Lanky Roy and Peaches, Lanky Roy's baby mother, had been telling people in the community that he was crazy because he talked to Mongrel. Even his classmates at school teased him about it. He looked at his dog friend. "She tell him that is after a hit mi head from the accident?" he asked.

"Nope," answered Mongrel. "A doubt the mailman would believe that after a bicycle accident, you able to understand animal talk."

Clifton touched the left side of his head and felt a long, thin, five-inch scar that ran from the middle of his head to the top of his left ear. "The next time a see the mailman, a going to—"

"Going to what?" asked Mongrel.

"Show him the scar, let him know that is after a hit mi head, when a fall on the road . . ."

He couldn't manage to say the rest of his words. He always had a hard time talking about his near-fatal accident three years ago. He sat up and ran a palm over the shinbone of his right foot, where it had been broken in two places. He flexed the ankle of the same foot that had also broken as well. The boy grimaced as a sharp pain erupted from the old injured ankle. He blinked tears from his eyes as he tried to erase the memory of the accident.

Mongrel moved closer to his human friend. "A sorry the accident leave you with that funny walk," he said, "but a glad you develop the animal- talking gift because you is the only human who care about mi."

Clifton smiled and scratched the top of the dog's head in a playful manner. "A don't like how Lanky Roy treat you, Mongrel, him have you from you was a puppy. You watch the yard day and night—"

"And the one time a fall asleep, the man almost starve mi to death," said Mongrel, shaking his head.

"Lanky shouldn't treat you like that because you always a bark," said Clifton, "and it work because it always scare the cokehead them from raiding the mango tree."

Mongrel nodded. "A remember when Lanky used to feed mi three times a day, with the good ole turn cornmeal and tin mackerel."

"A remember," said Clifton, "hot and fresh off the stove."

Mongrel shook his head. "And now, not even fishbone the man don't even throw give mi."

Clifton used his hand and rubbed his belly while he yawned big. "Talking about food make mi hungry like a dog." He looked at Mongrel and playfully poked the dog on its belly. "Is not you mi talking—"

Creeaakk. The noise of the two rusty old hinges on the front gate interrupted Mongrel and Clifton's conversation. They turned their heads toward the sound. They couldn't see the gate from where they were sitting because a young tangerine tree obscured their view. Clifton told Mongrel to stay where he was and tiptoed limply to the back wall of the house. He peeped around the wall, just in time to see Lanky Roy barge through the gate with great urgency. He watched as his uncle stopped halfway into the yard and started to look around.

"Is who?" asked Mongrel.

Clifton looked at his dog friend and put a finger to his lips. "Shhhh," he said. "Is Lanky."

*　　*　　*

At the front of the yard, the huge Rottweiler smelled Lanky Roy's scent. The dog opened his eyes, lifted his head, and made a lazy whining sound.

Lanky Roy rushed over to the doghouse and started to scratch the dog on its head. "Wad up, Putus, you miss mi?' he asked. Putus licked his master's hand and rested his head back on the ground.

*　　*　　*

At the back wall of the house, Clifton got down on both of his hands and knees. Like an injured crab, he crawled on his belly to the front wall of the house and stopped. He looked around the wall where he saw Lanky Roy talking to the half-sleeping huge dog.

"Don't worry, Putus," said Lanky Roy, "the time come for you to have the entire yard to youself." He brushed the hair on the back of the dog's neck with a hand. "All you have to do is just watch the yard 24-7. Make sure nobody don't come through the gate." He walked away, and then he stopped and turned to Putus, who had fallen asleep and was oblivious to his master's previous instructions. "And one more thing," said Lanky Roy, removing the slingshot from his waist and stretching the two pieces of rubber. "Look out for that thieving puss, a want you to rip him to shreds." He took a small bunch of keys out of his pants pocket and walked to the veranda. He pushed his hands through one of the diamond-shaped patterns of the veranda grille. He opened a padlock on the grille with one of the keys on the keyring and went into the house.

*   *   *

Clifton limped to the back of the house and told Mongrel what he saw and overheard.

Mongrel was unperturbed by the news. He smiled and looked at Clifton. "Listen, it obvious that Lanky kick mi to the curb for Putus," he said, "but him soon realize him mistake because the only thing that dog good at is sleeping."

"No, Mongrel," Clifton pleaded, "you should hear how the man sound, especially when him order Putus to kill Bruck Kitchen."

"Bruck Kitchen caused that on himself," said Mongrel, ignoring Clifton's grave concern. "A only surprise that is a slingshot Lanky hunting Bruck Kitchen with and not a gun."

Clifton was puzzled by Mongrel's comment. "What you mean?"

"You don't know what happen last night?" asked Mongrel. He was amazed that his human friend did not know about the incident that transpired.

"What happen last night? Remember mi go to bed early last night?"

"Oh yes, mi forget to tell you the drama," said Mongrel. "Last night, about 9:30, Bruck Kitchen climbed and squeezed through the kitchen window grille and eat off Lanky Roy steam fish out of him dinner plate."

"What, you not serious?" asked Clifton.

Mongrel laughed, showing a mouth full of rickety teeth. "A serious thing. Not even bone Bruck Kitchen don't leave in a the plate."

"Ohh, you never see smoke without fire. That's why him carrying that slingshot?"

"Yes, that's why him want to kill Bruck Kitchen," said Mongrel, stretching out his body on the warm ground. "Is not the first time Bruck Kitchen thieving out people food. Remember last week, him drink out Mass Gilbert, from next door, milk out a him bowl?"

"Oh yes, a remember now," said Clifton. "And a hear the milk was scalding hot. Lord, Bruck Kitchen thief bad."

"Bruck Kitchen is just like him thieving uncle Patah Puss. That's why Patah Puss did have to run away from the area, thieving run in Bruck Kitchen family."

"A true," said Clifton, "but back to the real issue. Lanky tell Putus that the time come for him to rule the yard alone, so that mean—"

Crupp! The back door of the house burst open. The sudden interruption caused both boy and dog to jump with fright. They looked toward the back door where they saw Lanky Roy and Peaches walking toward them. Peaches was one of the many dark-skinned people on the island that bleached her skin to look brown. Her face, hands, and neck had a pinkish-purple color due to the constant bleaching. Clifton did not like Peaches because she teamed up with Lanky Roy and treated him badly at times.

Whenever Clifton's mom—who was working in the United States—sent money for Clifton, Lanky Roy would give it to Peaches. She would mostly spend the money on herself and Tiffany—her and Lanky Roy's six- month-old baby girl. Clifton had never gotten a dollar of the money. Clifton watched as the unmarried couple walked to him and Mongrel. He noticed that his uncle had a long piece of rope in one of his hands.

Lanky Roy charged at Clifton, grabbed him by his left ear, and pulled him to his feet. "Little bwoy, look how long Peaches tell you to rake up the leaf from out the yard and clean up Putus's doo-doo?"

Clifton winced in pain as Lanky Roy pulled on his ear harder.

Mongrel turned his head away from the cruelty being inflicted on his friend.

"But a hungry," said Clifton, "and you and Auntie Peaches don't give we notting to eat—"

"We?" asked Lanky Roy.

"A mean, mi. You and she don't give mi notting to eat since morning and is after twelve now."

"Well," said Peaches, pointing a finger at him, "anytime you finish you yard work, you get some food. You round here a talk to the dog again?"

Lanky Roy turned to his baby mother. "A tired to tell people the bwoy mad." He looked at Clifton and let go of the boy's ear. "Go do what she tell you to do."

Clifton's left ear felt sore. He held on to it, picked up an old shovel that was lying on the ground, and limped off hastily to the front of the yard.

Lanky Roy looked at Peaches and wiped a bead of sweat from one of his eyebrows. "Babe, go and see if the bwoy doing what a tell him to do."

"Okay," said Peaches, "but a don't like the idea of you using Mongrel to tempt the crocodile."

"Relax, babe, that a the only way we can catch the croc," said Lanky Roy. He stooped down and attached the piece of rope that he had in his hand to the piece of rope collar around Mongrel's neck. "We just going put the dog near the river edge," he continued.

"And?" asked Peaches.

"And . . . and we hold the rope. When the croc climb out the water to get the dog, we stone it and kill it."

"Kill it?" asked Peaches.

"Yes, babe, pickney bath in some part of the river, a prefer kill it than it kill one of the pickney in the community—"

"Phonecard!" shouted an adult male voice at the gate.

"Somebody want phone card to buy," said Lanky Roy. "Go deal with it, a can manage here."

"Okay, Mr. Croc Exterminator," said Peaches, walking off to assist the person who had called.

All this time, Mongrel was wondering if his master was crazy. *How can Lanky use mi to tempt a crocodile? What if them don't pull mi away fast enough?* he wondered.

"Well, Mongrel," said Lanky Roy, snapping Mongrel out of his thoughts. "Time to put you retired body to use." He stood up from his kneeling position and walked to the front of the yard while pulling Mongrel behind him.

What is this on mi, Father God, it look like Clifton was right, Mongrel thought as he walked behind Lanky Roy. The helpless dog started to look around for Clifton to rescue him from his croc-bait predicament, but by the time he and Lanky Roy reached the front of the yard, Clifton was busy scooping up Putus's doo-doo with the shovel. Peaches was standing over the boy with a piece of stick in her hand like a slave master. She was also talking to an old man who looked like he was in his late sixties. The old man was dressed in dirt-stained khaki pants and a shirt. He had a large brown straw hat on his head and a tall pair of black water boots that reached below his knees. He gripped the wooden handle of a machete that he had in his right hand. The elderly man had an unpleasant look on his face.

"Sup, Farmer Brown, you all right?" asked Lanky Roy.

"No, man," said Farmer Brown, handing Peaches some money. "Them stray fowl and goat a give mi a hard time."

"Yeah?" asked Lanky Roy.

The old farmer nodded and took a phonecard that Peaches handed him. "Yes, the fowl them scratch and eat out all a mi corn grain that a plant yesterday."

"Sorry to hear that, and you work so hard in the hot sun," said Lanky Roy. "So what the goats them do?"

Farmer Brown waved his machete in the air. "Them stray goats, a going kill them because them eat down all a the suckers from around mi banana trees."

"Is not you alone complaining about stray animals, Farmer Brown," said Peaches. "Last Saturday night, a group a stray dog sleep and doo-doo right under the church crusade tent up the road. One fat load a dog doo-doo greet the pastor Sunday morning."

"A going fix them goat business," said Farmer Brown, scratching at the back of the phone card with the point of his machete.

While the humans were talking, Mongrel was trying to make eye contact with Clifton, but the boy was busy with his chores. "Clifton," he barked.

Clifton stopped what he was doing and looked at the dog, but Peaches quickly put the boy back to work by threatening him with the piece of stick that she had in her hand.

Lanky Roy looked at Mongrel and then looked at the old man. "Well, Farmer Brown, a can't stay with you, a have to go try catch that crocodile at the riverside."

"A crocodile in a the river?" asked Farmer Brown.

"Yes," said Peaches, "nobody don't know how him end up in there."

Farmer Brown shook his head. "What the hell you all saying to mi?" He looked to the sky. "Father God, we have stray fowl, stray goat, stray dog, and now stray crocodile. What next, stray locust to eat off all mi crop?"

"Good question," said Lanky Roy, pulling Mongrel toward the gate. "Anyway, them waiting on mi, Farmer Brown. A can't tarry."

Farmer Brown looked at Mongrel then at Lanky Roy, but before he could ask anything, Lanky Roy quickly pulled the dog through the gate and out into the street.

Mongrel clenched his teeth as the hot asphalt road burned his four paws. He quickened his pace and hurried behind Lanky Roy, who had started to run.

Sufferer, a brown and mangy-looking, old mongrel dog, was resting under a hibiscus tree on the roadside. He saw Mongrel running behind Lanky Roy with the long piece of rope around his neck. "Wh-what go-going on, Mongrel?" he panted, laboring with every breath because of his old age.

"A don't know, Sufferer, ask Clifton please!" shouted Mongrel while trying to catch up with Lanky Roy's running.

"Ahh right, when the sun c-cool down mi do it." The old dog shook a fly from its ear and watched as Lanky Roy pulled Mongrel in the direction of a shortcut at the bottom of the housing scheme.

*   *   *

Back at the riverside, the crowd of humans had gotten much larger. There were people from all over the community. Many of the people were on their cell phones, calling their friends and family members to come look at the crocodile in the river. There was even a local television news crew at the scene. A news cameraman was getting his camera ready to capture the rare event. A few other wannabe crocodile hunters were attempting to capture the reptile, which had moved a little farther out into the river. Yabba surveyed the crowd then looked at an old digital watch on his left wrist. "Why Lanky a take so long with the Mongrel dog, mon?" he grumbled to himself.

* * *

Up in the avocado pear tree, Bruck Kitchen observed the entire scene below. He was distracted by a noise that was coming from above. He looked up at the hot blue sky, where he saw War Plane, a loggerhead kingbird, known on the island as a pechary. War Plane was known to have a very short temper. He flapped his gray-and-black wings while chasing a black-feathered turkey vulture, known in the island as a John Crow. The John Crow's name was No-Shame. War Plane and No-Shame were the only two birds on the island that fought every day. No-Shame always got on War Plane's nerves, and War Plane would attack No-Shame by using his sharp beak to peck at the feathers in the vulture's back or his bald pinkish head.

Ignoring the ever-fighting duo, Bruck Kitchen returned his attention to what was happening at the riverside. He also noticed that, in addition to more humans at the riverside, there were also a few other animals present. "Them animals here is very brave," Bruck Kitchen whispered to himself.

* * *

Nanny Stush, a female goat that was of the Nubian breed, was standing several yards away from the human crowd. She had just moved to the area a month ago. Her light-brown-and-white hair had a silky sheen to it. She had two long white ears that distinguished her from the other goats in the community. A thin piece of rope hung around her neck and dangled between her front legs. Most animals in the Iron Bridge community described Nanny Stush as a stush and uptight individual who acted as if she were better than the rest of the animals in the community. It was rumored that she acted that way because she was born and bred at a popular goat farm from which most of the luxurious hotels on the island purchase their goat meat. The scorching midday sun had made her thirsty, so she had decided to get a drink at the river. When she saw the large crowd of humans at the riverside, she stopped at a distance and began to watch what was going on while she pretended to eat a few blades of grass.

* * *

Also on the riverbank that day was Jenny. Jenny was a domestic chicken, known on the island as a common fowl. Jenny was miserable and believed that she was in the same class as a New Hampshire hen. She had bright brown feathers and was one of the oldest hens in the Iron Bridge community. She had never hatched a chick before. She often blamed Clifton or a mongoose in the area for stealing her eggs, which meant she needed to change her nest from time to time. That day, she had believed that no one would expect her to be building a nest on the riverbank, so she had started to look for a nice and cozy spot to lay her daily egg. While Jenny was searching for a laying spot, she had seen the human crowd at the riverside. She decided to linger for a few minutes to see what had caused the herd of humans to gather there.

*   *   *

Grunty, an overweight, brown male pig, was cooling off in a mudhole beneath a hog plum tree a few yards downriver. Grunty had just filled his belly with some of the yellow mombin fruit that fell from the tree. He saw the large human crowd at the riverside, but he was too lazy to get up and get a closer look at what was going on. There was nothing more comfortable to Grunty than to eat a few hog plums and sleep during the day in his muddy Jacuzzi. The Hog Plum Day Spa and Dining, he called it. Ignoring the event happening at the riverside, Grunty closed his eyes and continued to soak up the cool, muddy water.

*   *   *

All of a sudden, there was uproar at the riverside among the humans. Everybody turned their heads toward the shortcut, where they all saw Lanky Roy running with Mongrel dragging behind. Yabba was relieved to see Lanky Roy. He ran halfway to meet his friend, taking the rope out of his hand and pulling Mongrel to the side of the river. Yabba kneeled in the muddy dirt while he secured the rope around Mongrel's neck. "What take you so long, mon?"

"That lazy nephew that a have up a the house, not doing him yard work," said Lanky Roy, "so a have to see to it that him do it."

"Okay, mon," said Yabba, standing up and brushing off his hands. "But the croc a get tired a the attention. Him already start to move away from the riverbank."

"Well, we have the mongrel dog now," said Lanky Roy, "so the croc should be more interested when we throw it to him as lunch."

Mongrel couldn't believe what he had just heard. *Throw to the croc!* The situation was worse than he had imagined. He looked toward the river where he saw the huge crocodile yawning, showing dozens of deadly teeth. Mongrel started to pull away from Yabba and Lanky Roy, but both men held on to the rope firmly. Lanky Roy grasped Mongrel by his collar and the skin of his lower back. He lifted the dog up and walked to the edge of the river.

The news cameraman, who had finished setting up his camera, ran toward Lanky Roy and Yabba with the camera on his right shoulder. He was determined to tape the unorthodox method of capturing the crocodile.

Mongrel looked around to see if Clifton was anywhere in the crowd, but his one and only human friend was nowhere in the riverbank. "Where is a friend when you need one?" Mongrel whispered. He looked at the crocodile that was still yawning in the murky river. Mongrel shook his head in dismay and started to sing the gospel song "Nearer, My God, to Thee" in his mind as Lanky Roy braced to throw him in the river.

*   *   *

Meanwhile, on the main road, a black BMW motorcar pulled to the left side of the road and parked behind a truck. The windows of the car were heavily tinted so no one could see inside. The driver opened a sunroof over his head and then wound down his window halfway. He lit a cigarette and began to watch the drama at the riverside.

*   *   *

At the riverside, some of the female humans shook their heads in disapproval. They did not like Lanky Roy and Yabba's decision to use a mongrel dog as bait in order to capture the crocodile. Several young male humans cheered them on with great enthusiasm. They were carrying on as if they were about to watch a movie with their favorite cartoon action hero. A male news reporter navigated the muddy riverbank and headed toward the cameraman just as Lanky Roy was getting ready to throw Mongrel in the river.

With Mongrel in both of his hands, Lanky Roy lifted Mongrel up, so his face was close to the dog's face. "When you see police or anybody who look like them will get you master in trouble, you must bark," he said to the dog.

Mongrel shook his head in disbelief. He couldn't believe his master was to going to throw him to a crocodile because he had fallen asleep when the police came to the house. He took one last look around to see if Clifton had come to rescue him, but his handicapped human friend was not among the rest of the humans.

Lanky Roy rocked his arms back and forth in order to build some momentum and then let go of Mongrel. The dog went flying ten feet in the air before gravity embraced him.

Like an out-of-control airplane, Mongrel's body spiraled toward the river.

He landed headfirst four feet from the crocodile with a loud splash. The crocodile turned its head to the spot where the dog had landed and started to glide slowly toward it. Mongrel briefly submerged but resurfaced and quickly swam out of the river in order to escape his demise.

Yabba immediately ran after Mongrel and caught the end of the water-soaked rope that was around the dog's neck. He dragged the wet and frightened dog back to Lanky Roy.

There was more cheering from the young male humans as Yabba pulled Mongrel to Lanky Roy. Some of the humans drew closer to the action with their cell phones in hand, recording the event.

Boosted by all the attention, Lanky Roy lifted up Mongrel for a second time and threw him in the air much harder than the first time. Mongrel went a few feet farther up in the air but fell much faster because of his water-soaked body and rope. That second time, Mongrel landed right on top of the crocodile's back. The impact of Mongrel landing on its back frightened the huge creature, and it reflexively snapped at Mongrel with its deadly jaws. The crocodile's sharp teeth missed Mongrel's neck but chopped off the rope collar with the long piece of rope from around his neck. With the long piece of rope in its mouth, the crocodile began to thrash about in a frantic mood.

Mongrel was happy that it was only the rope the crocodile had in its mouth and not a part of his body. He found some extra strength and swam away from the dangerous crocodile. He quickly swam to the other side of the river and arose from the water. He climbed onto an embankment and ran toward some bushes that were a few yards from the riverbank.

"Him getting away!" shouted one of the young male humans from across the river.

While Mongrel was running, several huge stones landed beside him. Without slowing down, he looked behind him and saw some of the young male humans throwing stones at him from across the river. One of the huge stones missed Mongrel by a fraction of an inch and hit the lower trunk of a nearby breadfruit tree with a loud thud. That horrific sound pushed Mongrel into maximum overdrive. He rushed to the bunch of bushes and dived into it, only to discover that it was full of thorns.

Blow wow, Mongrel thought, *a bad lucky to rahtid. A jump out a the frying pan and land right in the fire.* He was panting fast and hard. He ripped a few thorns from his body with his teeth. He peeped through the leaves of the prickled bushes and saw that none of the humans had dared to cross the river to look for him. He rested his head between his front paws and closed his eyes while he contemplated his next move.

*   *   *

At the riverside, Bruck Kitchen continued to watch from the top of the avocado pear tree. He looked down at Lanky Roy and Yabba. The two friends were standing at the river's edge, talking and pointing to the crocodile that was still in the water. Bruck Kitchen looked at the crocodile and shook his head. "If Lanky can dash him own dog to a crocodile," he murmured, "a can just imagine what him would do to mi who eat out him food." He cautiously began to make his way down the trunk of the avocado pear tree. "A not staying to find out what him would do to mi."

One of the humans on the riverbank shouted, "Lanky, why you never use a chicken instead?"

"A true, mon," said Yabba, turning to Lanky Roy. "A that a see them use on TV. The only thing is a dead chicken the man in the documentary use."

"Chicken?" said Jenny to herself. After Mongrel had crossed the river, Jenny had shaken her head in dismay at the stupidity of the humans. She had walked off and continued to look for a laying spot when she heard the human suggest that Lanky Roy use a chicken as bait. "A cannot stay in this area then, it don't safe," she said. She quietly tiptoed away from the river.

A little human boy saw Jenny and shouted, "See a chicken here!"

All eyes turned to the little boy who, in turn, pointed at Jenny. Yabba was the first human to run after Jenny while some of the teenage humans followed suit. Jenny took off upriver, at bird speed, with the humans chasing her. She tried to fly, but she ended up losing a few of her feathers instead; she was too old for that kind of stunt. To her left, she spotted a dead old tree trunk lying on its side, with a clump of bushes at the root. Jenny slipped under the tree trunk as quickly as she could and hid among the clump of bushes. Yabba and the teenage humans ran up to the dead tree trunk and stopped beside it. They all began to search for Jenny. One of the teenage humans pointed to the bunch of bushes and handed Yabba a long piece of stick. Yabba poked the bushes in order to flush Jenny out from her hiding place. He pushed the stick deeper into the clump of bushes, and a swarm of paper wasps flew out to him from the bushes. Scared of being stung, the rest of the humans scattered in all directions like cockroaches. Yabba dropped the piece of stick and accidentally fell backward on his back. He tried to evade the swarm of wasps by crawling backward on his buttocks. As he was about to get up, one of the wasps landed on his right ear and stung him. Yabba cried out in pain and fanned off the wasp with a hand. He got up and ran off after the rest of the humans with a dozen angry wasps zooming behind him.

*　　*　　*

While the humans were chasing Jenny, Bruck Kitchen was still trying to leave the riverside. He had just cleared the tall trunk of the avocado tree and leaped to the ground. He didn't even bother to head in the direction he came. He ran off downriver with a mad dash. While he was running, he saw Nanny Stush, the stush female goat. She was standing and looking as if she didn't realize what was taking place at the riverside. He stopped and looked at her. "Lady, you don't see what going on?" he asked.

Nanny Stush looked at Bruck Kitchen and turned away from him as if he didn't deserve her time. "Oh please, do you really believe those humans would throw me to that crocodile?"

Bruck Kitchen looked at her with a puzzled look on his face. "Lady, what planet you live on? You really think them humans care if you is a—"

"Listen to me, pussycat," said Nanny Stush, turning to face him. "My meat is the most expensive meat on the entire island. Do you really think those human hooligans would waste my mutton to feed a croc?"

Bruck Kitchen was about to answer her when he heard a group of humans running toward their direction.

"See a goat and a puss here!" shouted one of the humans, who was sporting dreadlocks.

Nanny Stush's eyes were wide open, and her mouth agape. "Did he say goat?" she asked.

"No, him say mutton, expensive mutton for the croc."

"Oh my god. I thought I was indispensable!" Nanny Stush wailed.

"Oh yeah?" said Bruck Kitchen. "If you stay here, them going dispense you to the crocodile. Run!"

Bruck Kitchen sped off downriver as if he was running on fire.

Nanny Stush ran daintily behind Bruck Kitchen with the thin piece of rope around her neck flopping between her front legs. Her right front hoof bumped on a tree root that was sticking out of the ground. She lost her balance and almost fell on her nose. She regained her balance and looked at her front hooves while still running. "Oh my god!" she cried. "My false hooves! I just put them on this morning."

"Lady, stop worry 'bout you false hooves and worry 'bout you life!" shouted Bruck Kitchen. The humans that were chasing them were a bit far behind, but Bruck Kitchen was running as if they were inches away from him. While he was running past the hog plum tree, he saw Grunty, the overweight pig, lying under the tree. "What you doing here, Grunty?" he said, still running. "You need glasses to see what going on?"

"Nooo, Brucky," said Grunty. "A leaving now. Worst that one in front is a dread, and dread don't like hog!" He stood up out of his mudhole as muddy black water dripped from his underbelly. He ran off like he was running for his life. He overtook Nanny Stush right away, but Bruck Kitchen was a good distance ahead of him. He looked behind him and saw that the dreadlocked human and the other humans were getting closer. While running and looking back, he unintentionally branched off onto a narrow dirt track that led to a nearby graveyard.

*　　*　　*

Bruck Kitchen did not realize that Grunty was no longer behind him. He just kept on running straight ahead. The direction he was running in led to a steep gully. By the time Bruck Kitchen saw the end of the road, it was too late. He could not stop fast enough. He went over the edge of the gully headfirst.

Nanny Stush was still running and looking down at her front hooves. By the time she realized that the road had come to an end, she was already over the gully. She sounded like a police siren as she screamed all the way to the bottom of the gully.

The dreadlocked human was first to reach the edge of the gully. He carefully watched his footing and looked down in the deep gully. Down below, all he saw were bushes and trees. He stepped back and told the rest of the humans that he saw the puss and the goat fall over the gully. The other humans refused to go after the animals due to an old rumor that there was a sinkhole at the bottom of the gully. The dreadlocked human also told them that he believed that the hog ran in the direction of the graveyard. One of the teenage humans in the group suggested that they should search the graveyard, but his suggestion was met with numerous objections from the others. None of the humans wanted to visit an old graveyard that had graves as far back as the eighteenth century. They all turned and headed back in the direction from which they came. They were all disappointed that the day's excitement was coming to an end.

*　　*　　*

Back at the riverside, the sun was less hot in the sky. Like white cotton candy, a thick wad of cumulus clouds drifted lazily over the river. The crowd was still large, but most of the excitement had faded. Lanky Roy and Yabba were resting under the avocado pear tree. Yabba was holding on to his injured ear, which had doubled its original size. The two men looked on as a group of professional crocodile handlers from the National Environment and Planning Agency (NEPA) in Kingston secured the crocodile's mouth with duct tape.

The men had managed to harness and pull the crocodile out of the water on to the riverbank. To keep the reptile calm, the men had used an old T-shirt to cover its eyes.

"Okay," said one of the crocodile handlers. "We need all hands on deck wit dis one."

"No problem," said another man.

They all got in position to lift the crocodile. It took six grown men to lift the large reptile off the ground. Two men were at the tail, two were at the abdomen, and two at the neck. They all grunted under the heavy weight as they carried the crocodile up the dirt road to the main road.

Like rats following a pied piper, all the curious onlookers, including the news team, followed the six crocodile handlers. Lanky Roy and Yabba got up from under the avocado pear tree and followed them as well.

*   *   *

On the main road, the driver of the black BMW motorcar saw the group of people coming. He took out a black baseball cap from the car's glove compartment and put it on. He checked himself in the left rearview mirror and pulled the peak of the cap low down on his face. He watched through the tinted windshield of the car as the six men secured the crocodile in the back of a pickup truck and drove off with it. He scrutinized the faces of the people who were all watching the news team packing up its equipment. After the news team drove away, the driver continued to scan the faces of the people who were still on the scene. He saw Lanky Roy and Yabba standing under a tall tree on the roadside. He felt a bulge on his right hip and opened his door to step out.

"Not now," said a voice from the back of the car.

Like an obedient dog, the driver closed his door, looked in the inside rearview mirror, and smiled at the person who had spoken. He patted the bulge on his right hip, started the car, and slowly drove off, leaving the group of people behind.

CHAPTER THREE

At the bottom of the gully, Bruck Kitchen had landed on top of a huge ant nest. He had just finished brushing dozens of black crawling ants off his gray-and-black fur. Some of the ants had even ended up in his ear and nose. He sneezed and looked around at his surroundings for the first time. Garbage was everywhere. Plastic bags and plastic bottles were lying all over the ground as if several humans had used the gully as their personal dumping ground. It was an eerie sight to him. The bushes and trees were so close together that he felt like they were closing in on him. The ground was uncomfortably damp, and the scent of decayed vegetation was strong in the air. He looked and listened to find out whether any of the humans had followed him to the bottom of the gully, but the only sound he heard was a cracking sound from above.

He looked up to see a large dry tree limb falling from its tree. The tree limb was plummeting right toward his head. He leaped out of the way as the dry limb crashed on the ground where he was standing. Thankful that he wasn't crushed to death, Bruck Kitchen was about to walk away when he felt something crumbling beneath his four paws. He looked down and saw that he was standing on a dry, rotten old crocus bag. Protruding from one end of the bag was a cat's skull. The skull's two empty eye sockets seemed to be staring at him. Bruck Kitchen was so frightened that his heart almost came out of his mouth. He sprang off the crocus bag, but one of his claws got caught in the bag and caused it to tear open. Several bones of a dead cat rolled out on the ground. The bones were clean and dry as if the cat had died a long time ago. A piece of red electrical cord was among the bones of the cat also. "My lawd," said Bruck Kitchen, "no, mon, a not spending one more second down here."

Bruck Kitchen looked around at the thick bushes and trees around him and realized that climbing to the top was the only way out of the gully. He started to make his way to the top when he remembered Nanny Stush.

He recalled hearing her falling after him, but he didn't know where she had landed. He thought about leaving her, but his heart wouldn't allow him to, so he decided to look for her.

"Hello, lady," he called out while keeping his voice down. He didn't want to make any unnecessary noise, just in case the dreadlocked human or any of the other humans decided to brave it and climb down into the gully.

"Where are you, lady goat?" Bruck Kitchen called out once more. He listened again for a response. Hearing no answer, he began to make his way stealthily up the steep incline of the gully. All of a sudden, he heard a faint sound coming from his right. He stopped and listened, but the sound did not sound like it was coming from a human. He quietly walked in the direction that he had heard the sound and tried not to make any noise on the damp earth beneath his feet. He heard the sound again, but this time, he could make out two words.

"Assistance please," said the voice. He discovered that the sound was coming from behind a six-foot-tall bunch of susumba trees that were off to his right. Careful not to be pricked by its sharp thorns, Bruck Kitchen watched his steps until he saw Nanny Stush. The goat was on top of an old, discarded mattress that was wedged between two of the susumba trees. Like an overturned beetle, she was lying on her back with her four feet in the air. The piece of rope around her neck was entangled in one of the susumba trees. "Assistance please," she called out again. Her voice was getting weaker because of the strain to her neck caused by the tangled rope.

Bruck Kitchen leaped on top of the old mattress. "Lady, you a the best," he said. He started to chew through the rope that was around Nanny Stush's neck. He took a break from his rope-chewing task and looked at her. "You dying, and before you holler out for help, you calling out *assistance please*. How you expect anybody to hear you that way?" He finished chewing through the last of the rope and spat out a few shreds of rope out of his mouth.

Nanny Stush struggled to her feet and flexed her neck and legs in order to regain some blood circulation. "I tried to call as loud as I could—"

"A not talking the volume a you voice," said Bruck Kitchen. "Next time, bawl out for help. You is a Jamaican. You can't chat patwah?"

Nanny Stush ignored his question. She didn't like it when anyone asked her that particular question. She wasn't fond of the Jamaican patois dialect; she thought it was a poor way of speaking. "Ewwww," she said, looking at the old mattress. "I can't believe I fell on that dirty thing."

Bruck Kitchen shook his head and laughed. "Lady, consider youself lucky; at least you fall on top of a mattress. I fall in a ant's nest—biting ants to make it worse."

"That's devastating," said Nanny Stush, making a disgusted face. She examined her body to see if there were any ants crawling on her.

"Devastating?" asked Bruck Kitchen. "It would be more devastating if a never hear you 'assistance please' calling."

"Why?"

"Because you would probly end up like that dead puss in that crocus bag over there."

Nanny Stush opened her eyes wide and looked at Bruck Kitchen. "Did you say dead?"

"Yes, dead, a matter of fact, him bone white," said Bruck Kitchen walking off. "And if we don't hurry up, we will both end up like him very soon. Come on."

"Yes, sir," she said, walking after him. "Where are we going?"

Bruck Kitchen stopped to listen if anyone was coming. "A sure there will be a emergency meeting at the cave."

"This evening?" asked Nanny Stush.

"Yes, Billy G, the president of the Animal Committee, will surely call a meeting before the day done."

"You mean that old goat?"

"Yes, him old, but him wise. A just have a strong feeling him going call a meeting."

"Wasn't there a meeting last Saturday?" asked Nanny Stush.

"Yes, the meeting normally keep every last Saturday," said Bruck Kitchen, walking faster. "But with today incident, a emergency meeting sure to keep. That is where a heading for now."

Nanny Stush quickened her pace behind him. "I have heard about the Iron Bridge Animal Committee, but I have never attended one of its meetings." She began to look around like she was getting scared. "Furthermore, I don't want to go through that old graveyard."

"Nothing is wrong with the grave—"

"Oh my god," she said, looking down at her feet. "All my false hooves are gone."

Bruck Kitchen stopped and turned around to face her. "You start that false hoof thing again?" He was starting to get annoyed by Nanny Stush's naivety. "Why you wear them false-clay hooves by the way?" he said, walking away from her.

"I wear them because they are fashionable."

"So some female humans wear false toenails, and you wear false hooves?"

"Yes, do you have a problem with that?"

"Nope," said Bruck Kitchen, "I have no problem with you fake hooves, lady."

"By the way, my name is Nanny, but some of those bad-minded animals call me Nanny Stush."

"A know," Bruck Kitchen laughed. He slowed down and waited for her.

Nanny Stush walked fast and caught up with him. "It's not funny. What is your name?"

"Bruck Kitchen, but most people call mi Brucky or Kitchen."

"That's an interesting name. Why do they call you Bruck Kitchen?"

"You ask more question than a lawyer. Is a long story why them call mi Bruck Kitchen."

"Okay, sir. Lord, I'm so tired, I could use a piggyback ride."

"Well, the only one who could give you a piggy ride is Grunty," said Bruck Kitchen, "but a sure Grunty is far away from this area by now."

They reached the top of the gully, and Bruck Kitchen started to look around to see if he saw any of the humans. After he saw that it was safe to walk out in the open, he turned to Nanny Stush. "You see that track there?" he asked, pointing with a paw in the direction of the track that Grunty had branched off on. "That track will carry we to the cave."

Nanny Stush looked toward the track and took two steps back. "But we would have to go through the graveyard, and I'm afraid of human ghosts."

"Look, lady, a mean, Nanny. There is no such thing as a ghost. Okay, which one you prefer? To see a human ghost or feed to a crocodile by a living human?"

Nanny Stush looked at her hooves. She was shaking a little in the knees. "A . . . ghost."

Bruck Kitchen stepped aside and used his right front paw to point in front of him. "Come, go in front, ladies before gentleman. Lead the way."

Nanny Stush just stood there looking at him. She didn't want to take the lead, and she didn't want to walk behind either. She would rather walk beside him, but the track looked like it was too narrow for both of them to walk beside each other.

"You know what, mi out of here," said Bruck Kitchen." He jogged across the open to the narrow track, leaving her standing, looking at him.

"Wait for me, Kitchen!" shouted Nanny Stush. She darted after him as Bruck Kitchen entered the narrow track.

CHAPTER FOUR

All the animals in the Johnson Lane Housing Scheme and the surrounding area were talking about Mongrel's unfair treatment. They had also heard that Mongrel was not the only animal the humans wanted to use as croc bait. All the stray dogs, cats, and fowls in the community were concerned about their safety. Even some of the white-feathered chickens, which a few of the humans raised to sell as meat, did not feel safe in their coops. The regular common fowls in the community were watching their backs. Some of them were already on their roosts, even though it was just minutes to two in the afternoon.

Lanky Roy was at his gate, removing a punctured spare tire from the trunk of his illegal taxi. The station wagon wasn't licensed to carry public passengers, but that didn't stop Lanky Roy from using it as a taxi during the evening rush hour. He turned to Yabba, who was standing close by. Yabba was rubbing a handful of green bush on to his swollen right ear.

"Can't believe Independence Day a come up," said Lanky Roy, handing Yabba the punctured spare tire. "And a don't have a battery for the ride to rahtid."

Yabba took the tire from Lanky Roy. "Well, a can fix the spare tire, but a can't fix the battery."

"Yeah, a know," said Lanky Roy, looking at the tires on the car. "But at least a have four good tire, and a working spare when you fix it."

"Don't worry, mon, a will ask one a mi customer if them have a second-hand battery to sell."

Lanky Roy looked at the dozens of green East Indian mangoes on the mango tree. "If the mango them was ripe, a could sell them and buy a battery."

"Yeah, but them green," said Yabba. He rubbed his chin while he thought of a solution. "You know what you can do, Lanky?"

"What?" asked Lanky Roy, looking at his friend.

"Try get some a the chemical that them fruit sellers use to force-ripe them mango."

"What chemical, and how that work?"

"Is a powder," said Yabba, "people call it carbide. Them wrapped it in a piece a cloth or old socks and put it in a box with the mango."

"A don't understand. How that force-ripe the mango?"

"It give off a strong heat and let the mango ripe extra fast, mon. Mi grandfather use to use it ripe banana. It make the outside a the banana yellow, but inside, no ripe good."

Lanky Roy closed the trunk of the car. "A don't care if the inside a the mango don't ripe, the outside people a look at. A would love some a this carbide powder. How a can get some?"

"A will ask around," said Yabba. "A hear you can buy it from somebody who work in a one a them place that sell chemical. Don't worry, we must find it."

"Okay," said Lanky Roy. "In the meantime, mi big-head sister a foreign supposed to send some money for Clifton this week."

"That sound good, mon."

Lanky Roy smiled and rubbed his hands together. "Yeah, a going put some a the money toward a battery."

"Don't get too excited, mon." Yabba laughed. "Remember that Peaches have to approve a that first."

"Approve what, a mi run things."

"Oh yes?" asked Yabba. "You remember the last time when you—"

"Look, just go fix the tire and shut up," said Lanky Roy, pushing Yabba playfully on the shoulder. "Street have ears."

Yabba lifted the punctured spare tire and rested it on one of his shoulders. "Okay, boss," he said, "a won't talk out you business to the scheme." He laughed at Lanky Roy while holding on to his throbbing ear.

Lanky Roy was not enjoying the teasing. "You better give God thanks that is you ears the wasp bite you on and not one a them lip."

"Why?" asked Yabba.

"Because it wouldn't be a pretty sight if you lip them get any bigger." Lanky Roy laughed.

"Laugh at mi same way, mon. One day a wasp going bite you."

"A don't afraid a wasp bite. When wasp see mi, them run."

"Okay, boss, a hear you. Later," said Yabba. He walked off with one hand, balancing the punctured tire on his shoulder.

Lanky Roy watched Yabba walking away, then looked at the green mangoes on the tree and smiled.

* * *

On the veranda of Lanky Roy's house, Tiffany, the six-month-old baby girl, was lying on her back in a white metal crib. She was smiling at a spinning plastic toy bird that was attached to the top of the crib. She cooed and snatched the toy while it played "Mary Had a Little Lamb."

Peaches sat close by in a white plastic chair. She was rubbing bleaching cream on her face from a large tube. As she applied the thick white cream to her two-toned face, she looked in a small mirror that she had in her lap. Dissatisfied with the first application, she squirted a large amount in her palm and started another dose.

The song from the plastic bird stopped, and its wings and head dipped in a dead silence. Peaches got up and wiped her hands on the orange spaghetti-strap blouse she had on. She examined the battery compartment of the musical toy and discovered that the two triple-A batteries inside had died.

Tiffany made a soft crying sound as if she were getting bored with the silence. Peaches attempted to lift her up in order to rock her to sleep but pulled back her hands suddenly. She remembered that she was handling bleaching cream and didn't want to touch the baby's delicate skin with her tainted hands. "Damn," she cursed silently. "A need two batteries for you bird, Tiffy."

She looked toward the gate and the front of the yard. "Clifton!" she shouted.

There was no answer from her baby father's nephew. She walked to the veranda and walked toward the back of the yard, calling out the boy's name while Baby Tiffany kicked up a storm in her crib.

*   *   *

With a dejected look on his face, Clifton stood at the edge of the river and watched an empty plastic bottle float by in the water. He had arrived at the riverbank to search for Mongrel after Sufferer, the mangy old dog, told him that he believed Lanky Roy had taken Mongrel to the river. When Clifton got to the riverbank, all he saw was a muddy riverbank and lots of human footprints.

Hunching on the ground beside Clifton was White Squall, a male cattle egret, known on the island as a gawling. The bird had long, greenish-yellow legs and a full body of white feathers. The bird had just finished describing in full length what took place at the river earlier in the day.

Heartbroken by the horrible news, Clifton was even more concerned than before. "A hope him not injured," said Clifton.

"Mongrel is aright, Clifton," said White Squall. "A tell you already that him make it across the river safe."

Clifton looked at the tall bird with a glimmer of hope in his eyes. "You sure?"

"Of course a sure, a was here before it start," said White Squall, pecking at the feathers on his back with his yellow bill. "A was supposed to meet a heifer cow here to pick some ticks off her back."

"A guess you never get to meet her then."

The cattle egret shook its head. "Nope, all hell pop loose before that, but Mongrel manage to swim cross and run in some bush."

"Well, a guess a can only pray him is okay," said Clifton, looking across the river. "If you see him, tell him that a miss him . . . tell him to come home."

"Okay, a will, but a doubt Mongrel want to come anywhere near Lanky Roy after today."

"Well, a understand. Still give him the message."

"Don't worry," said White Squall. "If a see Mongrel, a will give him you message. Go home and rest you brain."

Clifton tried to look cheerful by forcing a smile. "Thanks, White Squall, a appreciate you help."

"No problem. A heading to mi nest to get a quick nap, so later."

Clifton said good-bye to the bird and walked back to his home as he tried to figure out a way to help his fugitive canine friend.

CHAPTER FIVE

Whether it was the fear of being thrown in the river to the crocodile or fear of the dreadlocked human catching him, Grunty, the pig, had made the graveyard look like a racetrack. He had even knocked down a few old headstones in the process while he sprinted away from the pursuing humans. One would wonder how a fat, oversized pig could run that fast.

He had cleared the graveyard and several prickled trees and was Zigzagging through an area that the animals and birds called the Fruit Basket. The Fruit Basket was an area that had all types of fruit trees that the animals, insects, and birds ate from. There were fruit trees like sweetsop, guava, guinep, banana, and lots more. There was even an old guango tree, and a few stray cows in the community would visit to eat the black pods that fell from its branches.

To the animals and birds in the community, the Fruit Basket was like heaven on earth. Sometimes, birds would fly from other parishes on the island to eat there. Food from the Fruit Basket was in abundance all year round. Thorny trees of all sorts, both large and small, protected the perimeter of it.

Most of the humans knew of the Fruit Basket, but they all avoided the area. There was a human cokehead in the community called Pickah, who would often go around and steal people's fruit from their trees. One day, Pickah had penetrated the numerous prickly trees of the Fruit Basket and stole most of the ripe fruits from the trees. Billy G, the president of the Animal Committee, had suggested during one of the committee meetings that he believed there should be at least two large wasp nests in each fruit tree, just in case the cokehead or another human decided to steal the fruits again. All the other animals agreed with Billy G's suggestion, so he gave Stinger, the leader of the wasps, the go-ahead to construct the nests in the trees. One week later, there was at least one wasp nest on each branch of the fruit trees.

Pickah, who had returned two weeks later for a second crop reaping, got several bites from some of Stinger's angry wasp thugs. He ran from the Fruit

Basket with his face as fat as an overinflated tire tube. Neither he nor any other humans, was ever seen in the Fruit Basket area again.

*   *   *

As the warm evening sun kissed the contours of the land below, a loud pecking sound could be heard, coming from a coconut tree that was close to the Fruit Basket. Jack Hammer, a Jamaican woodpecker, pecked a hole in the upper trunk of the coconut tree. He was given the nickname Jack Hammer because of the noise his strong beak made whenever he was drilling a hole for a nest in a tree. From his position on the trunk of the coconut tree, Jack Hammer watched Grunty zigzagging through the Fruit Basket with lightning speed. He shook his head and resumed his home building, wondering what could have gotten in that crazy pig.

*   *   *

Dashing through the Fruit Basket at top speed, Grunty reached an area where there were several banana trees. He almost tripped over one of the banana trees that had fallen in the road. As he regained his balance, he heard a voice call out to him.

"Wait, is who that, Grunty!" shouted the voice.

The voice sounded familiar to Grunty, so he tried to make a sudden stop, which caused his legs to make four long skid marks in the dry loose dirt. He finally came to a stop when he crashed headfirst into one of the banana trees. The banana tree was almost uprooted by his heavy weight and the speed he was going.

Grunty quickly got up off the ground, but he was a bit dizzy from crashing into the banana tree. He shook the dizziness from his head and tried to pretend as if everything was okay. He was also breathing very heavily. He turned around and looked where the voice had come from. He realized that the voice had come from his friend, Jacko.

Jacko was a popular spider in the community who loved to jive his friends. It was known that if you couldn't take a little jiving, you couldn't be friends with Jacko or hang around him. The funny thing was, Jacko liked to jive others, but he didn't like to be jived by anyone. He was not good at taking a taste of his own medicine. Despite his jiving ways, Jacko was one of the first people to come up with a solution to a problem—none of which he volunteered to do. Jacko, who planted a few crops on a small plot of land near the Fruit Basket, was tired from the day's work. He lowered a bunch of ripe banana that he was carrying on his shoulder to the ground and wiped a streak of sweat from his forehead with one of his eight legs. He looked at his pig friend, who looked like he was badly in need of a mudhole.

"What's up, Jacko?" asked Grunty. He was still breathing heavy and was trying hard to catch his breath.

"Rahtid," said Jacko. "Then how you blowing like Hurricane Ivan so, papa?"

Grunty walked to a large guango tree that was close by and laid down under its broad, cool shade. He gave his breathing a few minutes before he answered Jacko's question.

"Jacko, a piece a excitement just take place at the river. A have to gallop from the area fast."

"Excitement?" asked Jacko, lifting the bunch of ripe banana and carried it to the guango tree. He leaned it against the tree's flaky bark and sat beside Grunty. "Then is excitement, why you run so fast till you almost level every banana tree in the area?"

"Hold on, Jacko, you don't understand—"

"You right, a really don't understand," said Jacko, "because every Jamaican a know love excitement, you is the first one a see running from it."

"No, this is what happen," said Grunty. He went on to describe the day's incident to Jacko. After he was finished, Jacko was trying not to laugh while trying to be serious about the situation at the same time.

"No man, that is not excitement, Grunty. That is call animal cruelty. A hear the humans have some kind of law against it."

Grunty nodded. His breathing was returning to its normal pace. "Yeah, real cruelty. No animal don't deserve that kind a treatment from no one, whether from a human or a another animal."

"A thought Lanky Roy forgive Mongrel about that drop-a-sleep issue long time."

"Apparently not," said Grunty, removing a thorn that was attached to the hair on his face. "If him never thief the people electricity, police couldn't lock him up, is not Mongrel fault."

Jacko looked at the single thorn that Grunty had removed from his facial hair. "Then is how come you run through so many prickle and is only one jook you papa?"

Grunty replied, "Jacko, a was moving so fast, prickle barley have time to jook mi."

"You right," said Jacko, pointing to the banana tree that Grunty had accidentally knocked over. "Because that banana tree is a true testament to you speed."

"Yeah, a was going hard." Grunty laughed. "Poor Nanny Stush, a can't stand her heighty-tighty ways, but a did feel sorry for her when the humans was running down she and Bruck Kitchen."

"A hope them get away," said Jacko, "I can't believe that Nanny Stush really a talk to one a we, especially talking to Bruck Kitchen. Where is both of them?"

"A don't know where them turn off," answered Grunty, shaking his head. "But all I know is, when that banana tree stop mi, them was never behind mi. I not even know when a come through the graveyard."

"You right," said Jacko, "you run so fast till you run pass you yard."

"A not even did realize. A just never want that dread bwoy to catch mi."

"A can just imagine if him did catch you," said Jacko. Anyway, you run in the right direction. When Billy G hear about this, him going call a emergency meeting—"

"You hear that sound?" asked Grunty. Both of his ears were perked up in the air like an old-time TV antenna.

"What sound?" asked Jacko, looking in all directions. "The only sound a hear is Jack Hammer drilling."

They both looked toward a small track that led from a bunch of prickled trees to the guango tree. Nanny Stush and Bruck Kitchen walked out from the bunch of prickled trees and walked toward them. The stush female goat was walking slowly in front of Bruck Kitchen. Her long ears hung from the sides of her head like two withered pumpkin leaves. Bruck Kitchen walked closely behind her while constantly looking behind him.

Jacko looked at Nanny Stush. Even though Grunty had told him that she and Bruck Kitchen had run in the same direction, he definitely wasn't expecting to see them together, especially with Bruck Kitchen's thieving reputation. *The day is getting more unbelievable as it go by,* he thought.

Bruck Kitchen saw Grunty and called to him. "Wait, Grunty, you end up far. You not even stop to see if mi and Nanny Stush—a mean, if me and the lady was okay." He and Nanny Stush reached the guango tree. Nanny Stush laid down beneath the large tree and started to remove dozens of thorns, with her teeth, that was stuck to her hairy skin.

"Sorry, Brucky," said Grunty, "but when a took off, a decide that a not looking back like Lot's wife."

"And knowing how you can run fast," said Bruck Kitchen.

"A telling you, man, a was more flying than running," said Grunty, "to how fast a was going, a run pass mi yard. Ask Jacko if you think a lying."

Bruck Kitchen turned to his spider friend. "Hey, what's up, Jacko? Long time a don't see you, man."

"To rahtid, Brucky," said Jacko, "and look under what circumstances we meet up, eh?"

"Bwoy, it rough," said Bruck Kitchen, "especially on Mongrel. Mi sorry for him, but a couldn't help him. Lanky want mi dead or alive."

"Mi hear 'bout the steam-fish episode." Jacko laughed. He turned to Nanny Stush. "And isn't this the famous Nanny Stush?"

"Oh please," said Nanny Stush. "I'm sure after today, that poor mongrel dog will be more famous than me."

Jacko laughed. "You right, because from what I hear, them need to put Mongrel in the *Guinness Book a World Record.*"

"Why?" asked Grunty.

"Because him supposed to be the first dog who cheat death two time in less than five minutes," said Jacko.

Grunty and Bruck Kitchen laughed at Jacko's take on Mongrel's situation. Even Nanny Stush could not avoid a chuckle.

"Anyway," said Bruck Kitchen after the laughing had subsided. "A believe we all should head over the cave now."

"A was just telling Grunty," said Jacko, "that a believe Billy G going to go call a emergency meeting this evening, a not waiting on Mouth-a- Massi announcement."

Mouth-a-Massi was a Jamaican black-billed, green-feathered parrot. He was given the nickname Mouth-a-Massi because he liked to talk a lot. Sometimes, the birds and animals could hear Mouth-a-Massi's mouth from dusk till dawn, especially when he found a marijuana field and ate a few seeds from one of the marijuana buds. Eating the marijuana seeds always made him high, and he would choose to perch on the tallest tree and make a lot of noise. He was once a pet parrot, but his human owners threw him out because they could not sleep at night with his constant squawking. One day, they got fed up and threw both Mouth-a-Massi and his cage out of their house. When the cage hit the ground, the gate fell off, and Mouth-a-Massi flew away to the Fruit Basket. That day, the animal community's tranquility was shattered.

Jacko had suggested to Billy G that he thought it would be a good idea to capitalize on Mouth-a-Massi's chatty ways and make him the one to announce to the animal community when there was going to be a meeting. Billy G had taken Jacko's advice and appointed Mouth-a-Massi as the official announcer. Mouth-a-Massi was like a flying PA system. He always performed his job with great enthusiasm because it provided him with the perfect opportunity to chat and make noise.

"I believe we should not wait on that chatterbox announcement too," said Nanny Stush, "because when we were walking over—a mean, I don't know if it was my imagination because I was scared, but I kept hearing sounds in the bushes behind us."

"Come on, Ms. Nanny." Jacko laughed. "Is because you never walk through the graveyard before. Don't be such a coward, you have to be very brave in these times."

Grunty's ears were perked up once more. There was a strange sound coming from a bunch of dry bush that was a few yards away from the guango tree. It sounded like human footsteps. Jacko was the first one to run and hide. He scuttled up the trunk of the guango tree. He didn't even remember his bunch of ripe banana. In less than ten seconds, he was at the very pinnacle of the tree, looking down at the others struggling to find a hiding place.

Grunty jumped up off the ground and accidentally tripped over Nanny Stush as he tried to run in the opposite direction of the footsteps.

Bruck Kitchen leaped and squeezed between the bunch of ripe bananas and the trunk of the guango tree, leaving Nanny Stush out in the open.

Nanny Stush scrambled to her feet and started to turn in circles. She was confused; she couldn't figure out where to hide. She finally ran and hid behind the thick trunk of the guango tree. She was shaking like a leaf on a windy day. Her four knees were shaking with nervousness.

* * *

Grunty had found a hiding place under a large pile of dry banana leaves among the banana trees. He laid flat on his stomach while he held his breath like a professional free diver. He was too scared even to take a slow, shallow breath.

* * *

Behind the bunch of ripe bananas, Bruck Kitchen peeped toward the sound of the footsteps in the bushes. He suddenly realized that if the human that was approaching decided to steal the bunch of bananas, he or she would see him behind it. There was no time for him to try and find another hiding place; it was too late. He began to tremble with fright.

Out of the bushes came Guana, a Jamaican giant anole lizard, known in the island as a green lizard. Guana had bright green skin and was about twelve inches long. He lived in a large apple tree in the Fruit Basket and could be often seen on its smooth trunk. His friends had given him the nickname Guana because he looked like a small iguana lizard. Guana was a chameleon wannabe;

he would often boast to the other lizards and animals in the community that he had the ability to camouflage like an actual chameleon—something he had yet to prove to them because a Jamaican green lizard can only change from green to darkish brown.

Guana surveyed the area and spotted the bunch of ripe bananas. He wasn't a big fan of ripe banana, but the sight of the long ripe yellow fruit made him hungry. He walked toward the bunch of banana just as Bruck Kitchen stepped out from behind it. Guana was so frightened by Bruck Kitchen's sudden appearance; he almost ran up the guango tree.

"Guana, you footstep sound like human footstep you know, man," said Bruck Kitchen.

Guana smiled; he felt relieved that he was not the only one who was spooked. "Mi footstep doe sound like no human footstep, man."

"Sound exactly same way, you almost give everybody a heart attack."

Guana looked around to see what "everybody" Bruck Kitchen was talking about. "Everybody?" he asked.

As if on cue, all the others started to come out of their hiding places one by one. Nanny Stush slowly emerged from behind the tree trunk. Grunty walked up to them with a piece of dry banana leaf stuck behind his right ear. Nanny Stush saw the piece of dry leaf and pointed out to Grunty that it was behind his ear. Grunty thanked her and removed it by flashing his head sideways.

Jacko was the last one to reach the group. He slowly climbed down from the tree, looking a little embarrassed. Grunty, Nanny Stush, and Bruck Kitchen all looked at him. He quickly tried to divert their attention away from his lack of bravery by starting to jive Guana. "Wait, Guana, is you step through the bush so, like you is a ground lizard?"

Guana didn't like to be jived by Jacko, so he tried to stop Jacko before he went any further. "Doe bother with the foolishness, Jacko, mi is not any ground lizard, a tired to tell you, mi is like a chameleon."

Jacko said, "Yes, but a chameleon move with stealth, you know, creep up on them, pray without sound. A while ago when you a walk through the bush, we could stay a Montego Bay and hear you footstep."

Guana looked like he was about to change color; he was trying hard not to get angry. "Look here man, cut out the antics, you hear—"

"All right, boss, a stop," said Jacko. He didn't want his lizard friend to burst a blood vessel. "Anyway, what you up to?"

"Is over the cave a want to reach."

Jacko laughed. "Then is when you planning to reach, papa, if is walk you going to walk?"

"Look here, man," said Guana, "a doe like when people assume. A decide to come out here 'cause a was hoping to find a cow to hitch a ride on him or her back."

Grunty laid down on the ground and rested his head against the trunk of the guango tree. "Well, as you see, none a the cow in the community not here. You out a luck, Guana."

Guana sighed deeply. "Bwoy, a would even take a ride from Hebrew now," he said, referring to a humble and kind female donkey.

Jacko looked at Bruck Kitchen and Grunty and then looked at Guana. "Guana," he said, taking a step to him. "Hebrew get chase last week by two human cow thief. She hardly leave her yard from that."

Nanny Stush put a hoof to her mouth. "Oh my god," she said with wide-opened eyes. "Is the first I'm hearing this. I have never met her, but I heard she is a nice donkey. Is she okay?"

"Yes, she okay," said Grunty. "She escape, she is just a little embarrassed."

"I can just imagine," said Nanny Stush. She shook her head sideways and sighed deeply. "I can't believe that the humans are killing donkeys for their meat."

"Yes, a pure a that taking place on the island from the other day," said Bruck Kitchen. "Them kill the cow and donkey and mix the two meat. The human beef lovers can't tell the difference between the two meats."

"That's horrible," said the stush female goat. "Poor Hebrew. I don't know her, but I can relate to how she must have felt. Killing donkeys, oh my god."

"I wonder if is the same humans in the community doing these things?" asked Grunty.

"I have no idea where them two cow thief come from," said Jacko. "The only thing a can say about them is, them did desperate bad."

"Why is that?" asked Nanny Stush.

"Because Hebrew is so skinny," said Jacko. "A don't know where them would find meat on her to make patty."

Both Kitchen and Grunty laughed at Jacko's comment, but Nanny Stush didn't quite get the joke. "What do you mean?" she asked.

"Darling, when you meet Hebrew, you will see what a mean," said Jacko. "Hebrew is pure skin and bone. She more look like a donkey frame than a donkey."

Nanny Stush bit down on her bottom lip and tried to hide a smile. "You're something else. Not all of us were born to be fat. I hope she feels better now."

"A hope she come to the meeting tonight," said Jacko, "because a need to hear the full story from the horse's mouth, in this case, the donkey's mouth."

"True word," said Guana, looking at Jacko. "As a was saying, a heading for the cave because a hear the crocodile bite off one a Mongrel back foot and Billy G must call a meeting for that."

Grunty, Bruck Kitchen, and Jacko looked at each other, then looked back at Guana, as if he was crazy.

"One of his feet?" asked Nanny Stush. Her eyes looked like they were about to pop out of her head.

With Nanny Stush asking him a question directly, Guana was caught off guard. He wasn't used to talking to the proud and cocky female goat. He tried to recoup and gather his words. "Um . . . yes, a hear that when Lanky Roy dash Mongrel in the river the second time, the crocodile bite—"

"Who tell you that foolishness, man?" asked Bruck Kitchen. "A was on the scene and Mongrel get away and bolt on all four foot."

Guana looked confused as he tried to explain himself. "Is so Kas Kas said it happen, is she give mi the news."

Kas Kas was a stray female pigeon. She was notorious for her news-carrying ways. Kas Kas would often spread rumors and carry the wrong news to get attention. Her news-carrying ways would often land her in a heated argument with the other animals and birds, but that still didn't stop Kas Kas from spreading rumors.

"Come on, Guana, you know Kas Kas is very lie," said Jacko, turning to Nanny Stush. "She don't need to hear a full story, she just want to hear piece. Kas Kas is so lie, a wouldn't ask her the time a the day."

Bruck Kitchen and Grunty laughed at Jacko's description of Kas Kas's personality. Jacko was pleased that no one had joked about him running up the guango tree. He decided that he needed to keep talking to keep their minds on the current situation. "Anyway," he said, taking on the role of a group leader, "a think we need to head over to the cave right now."

Bruck Kitchen looked up in the sky at the evening sun that was creeping toward the western part of the island. "I agree, as you blink, night come."

Nanny Stush rested her head on a patch of green grass on the ground. "Lord, I am so hungry."

Jacko looked around at all of them. They all looked like they could eat something. He pointed at the bunch of ripe banana that was still leaning against the trunk of the guango tree. "If you all want a finger a ripe banana, you all can take one."

Grunty quickly bit off a finger of ripe banana and ate it all, including the skin of the fruit.

All the others each bit off a finger and began to eat.

Bruck Kitchen, who didn't eat ripe banana unless he was hungry, ate only half of his.

Nanny Stush ate hers delicately and slowly. She looked away from the other animals shyly while she ate.

Guana ate his like a human baby toying with its food. Both the jiving from Jacko and the discovery of Kas Kas's lie had caused him to lose his appetite.

"Okay, people, mealtime is up," said Jacko, turning to Guana. "Guana, a think it best if you hitch a ride on the bunch a ripe. A going carry it on mi shoulder."

"No problem," said Guana. He stepped back a few feet, ran, and leaped into the air, then landed on the bunch of bananas.

"Blow wow," said Jacko. "Guana, you is not only a ground lizard, you is also a flying lizard too!"

"You come back with that ground lizard foolishness again?" asked Guana.

Grunty laughed at Guana and watched as Jacko lifted up the bunch of bananas with the green lizard on top of it.

Jacko rested the bunch of bananas onto his left shoulder and started to walk toward a thick clump of bushes and trees. The other animals followed behind him. Bruck Kitchen overtook Jacko and took the lead.

Jacko looked at the housebreaking cat in front of him. "Yes, Brucky, you guard the front. Grunty, you guard the back."

"Yes," said Bruck Kitchen, "because if we hear bush mash, we know who first will run—"

"Eh ehm ehm," said Jacko, clearing his throat in order to avoid Bruck Kitchen from going any further.

From the sky above, they heard a loud noise. They all looked up and saw Mouth-a-Massi, the public announcement parrot, flying over the treetops. He was advertising his beak away. "Emergency meeting at the cave, starting in thirty minutes, everybody must attend!" shouted Mouth-a-Massi at the top of his voice.

"Wait, a now Mouth-a-Massi announcing this?" asked Bruck Kitchen. "Him behind time bad."

They all laughed as they walked farther into the thick bushes toward the foot of a hill that led to the cave.

CHAPTER SIX

The hot steam rose from the delicious turn cornmeal and tin mackerel Mongrel was eating. He licked his mouth and devoured the hot meal as if his life depended on it. As soon as he finished eating all the food in his food pan, his loving friend, Clifton, would refill the pan with more food. The strange thing was, the more food he ate, the hungrier he got.

His meal was interrupted by Mouth-a-Massi's yapping beak overhead. Mongrel couldn't make out what the talkative parrot was saying, but he didn't care because he was still hungry. He tried to concentrate on his food, but Mouth-a-Massi's voice was getting louder and louder. Mongrel looked up in the sky, just in time to see the parrot skydiving toward him. Mouth-a-Massi landed on top of Mongrel while clawing at the dog's back with his sharp claws. "The crocodile send mi for you!" he shouted in the dog's ear.

Mongrel tried to get the crazy parrot off him by rolling over onto his back. He felt a prick to the side of his head by a sharp thorn. He winced in pain, jumped to his feet, and looked around. There was no Mouth-a-Massi on his back or in the bush beside him. There was no Clifton or pan with food either. Mongrel had been dreaming. He felt the side of his head where the thorn had stuck him. He realized he had fallen asleep in the prickled bush when he was trying to figure out what he was going to do. Still rattled by the horrifying dream, he crawled out from under the bunch of prickled bush. All his joints and muscles felt stiff, so he stretched both of his front legs and then his two hind legs. His empty stomach made a weird growling sound as it protested for food. He looked up at the sun and figured he must have fallen asleep for about an hour and a half because the sun had drifted away from the river and was moving closer to the west.

Overhead, Mouth-a-Massi was announcing that there was going to be an emergency meeting in thirty minutes. "It better if a go to this meeting and hear what Billy G have to say," said Mongrel to himself. He figured attending the meeting would be the best move for him. He knew he was the main reason Billy G had called for an emergency meeting.

Never in his life had Mongrel thought that he would be so important. It seemed as if the Iron Bridge Animal Committee was calling a meeting because of his well-being. He couldn't wait to hear what the president of the Animal Committee had to say about his situation.

Even though he was hungry from both the dream and from not eating anything since the start of that day, Mongrel decided that he needed to head over to the cave as soon as possible. Maybe there would be a little food there like the last meeting he attended; maybe his best friend, Clifton, would be there. He wasn't sure if either of the two would happen, especially the latter, but the only thing he had at that moment was hope. As the saying goes, a drowning man catches at a straw. Hope was Mongrel's only straw. He looked around to make sure it was safe. After seeing that the coast was clear, he started the hungry journey to the cave. Poor Mongrel, if he only knew that what happened at the riverside that day was only the beginning.

CHAPTER SEVEN

The afternoon was getting cool in the Johnson Lane Housing Scheme. Halfway into the scheme, a few of the humans' children were playing in the street. The girls were on the sidewalk playing a game of dandy shandy, and the boys were playing soccer in the middle of the road. One of the human boys saw Sufferer, the mangy old dog, resting under a flowering tree that was close to the side of the road, and he kicked the soccer ball at the dog. The ball rolled and slammed into the old dog's left side. Sufferer quickly got up and scrambled off toward the entrance of the scheme, where he knew there would be a male human selling jerk chicken on the roadside. He was hoping to find a few chicken bones that were thrown away by some of the humans who usually bought and ate their jerk chicken on the spot. He also knew that other stray dogs in the area would be heading for the same jerk chicken spot as well. He walked as fast as he could while constantly looking behind him for any more malicious human attackers.

*   *   *

Lanky Roy was at his gate, leaning over the hood of the Toyota Corolla station wagon while he examined the vehicle's battery. "A need a battery bad," he grumbled to himself as he scraped off corrosion from one of the battery's terminals with a flathead screwdriver.

The rusty hinges on the front gate creaked. He turned his head to the gate and saw Peaches. She held Baby Tiffany with both hands and pushed the gate closed with her right hip. She walked up to Lanky Roy with a long face. "Why you turn off you phone?" she asked.

"Turn off?"

"Yes, you sister in the US was trying to reach you." She removed an iPhone from the back pocket of the pair of jeans she was wearing and showed the received call to Lanky Roy.

"Shooks," said Lanky Roy. He took out an old flip cell phone from his shirt pocket and looked at the screen. "The battery dead babe, that's why, it want charge."

"A hear you."

Lanky Roy noticed her long face. He knew that the only time she wore that look on her face was when something was not happening in her favor. "What the problem?" he asked.

"You sister said to tell you, she lose her job. She say she won't able to send money for Clifton this week or anytime soon."

The screwdriver fell out of Lanky Roy's hand onto the ground; he could barely move. He leaned back on the front of the car as he absorbed the shocking and disappointing news. "Ahh bwoy," he said, shaking his head. "And mi was depending on the money to buy a car battery, you know. Independence Day a come up an a need to do some taxi work."

"Don't forget the landlord rent due in one week," said Peaches.

Lanky Roy sighed. "And we invest this month rent in them four second-hand tire on the car."

"Well, you should know that the battery was going to dead before you buy the tires."

Peaches was getting on his nerves; he felt she was blaming him for their sudden bad luck. "Look here, don't—how a was supposed to know the idiot battery was going dead?"

Baby Tiffany made a soft cry and began to suck at her right big finger. Peaches looked at the baby and then looked at her baby's father. "And Tiffy need diaper too, a send Clifton at the shop to buy a pack."

Lanky Roy scratched his head as he thought about his situation. "A can't call Joyce, 'cause she expect mi to have this month rent. What a going do now?" he asked.

"You is the man of the house, Lanky," said Peaches. "Just remember you have three hungry mouth to feed now." She cradled Baby Tiffany onto her left shoulder and walked off, leaving Lanky Roy still scratching his head.

"Where you going?" asked Lanky Roy.

Peaches stopped and switched Baby Tiffany to her other shoulder. "A going to look for Clifton," she said. "Him taking too long at the shop, and a need to collect a DVD from Sandra, a don't want she scratch it." She looked up the road and saw one of her female friends and called out to her. She held Baby Tiffany against her shoulder and walked away from her baby's father.

Lanky Roy picked up the screwdriver off the ground and resumed working on the corroded battery terminal. He tried to focus on what he was doing, but he kept thinking about the money he would no longer be getting from his sister in the USA. What Peaches had said to him about him being the man of the house made him start to worry. *A have to make some money one way or the other,* he thought.

The sound of footsteps behind him interrupted his thoughts. He turned around and saw Pickah, the fruit-thieving cokehead, standing a few feet from the car.

Pickah was dressed in a dirty old blue sleeveless shirt and a pair of black jeans that were cut off at both knees. On his feet, he had on a worn-out, dirty pair of tennis shoes. Like roots of ginger sticking out of a kitchen basket, both of his little toes were sticking through a hole at the side of each shoe. He had an empty black plastic bag in one of his hands. "Whad up, Lanky?" he said, glancing at the East Indian mango tree in the front of Lanky Roy's yard. "You want mi wash di ride?"

"Wash which ride?" said Lanky Roy, closing the hood of the car. "Is mi mango tree you mapping out?"

Pickah shook his head while he looked toward the tall ackee tree at the back of the yard. "No, man, doe say dhat."

Lanky Roy walked up to Pickah while fanning him away as one would do to an annoying fly. "Move from mi gate. Move!"

Pickah did not budge; he stood his ground. The cokehead was determined to get two of the green mangoes from the tree to sell. A well- loaded East Indian mango or ackee tree was the biggest temptation for him.

"Boss, beg you, two a di mango, a—"

"All right, Pickah," said Lanky Roy. "You want two mango, see two mango here." Lanky Roy rested the screwdriver he had in his hand on top of the car's hood, reached into one of his pants pockets, and removed a shiny black marble. He then removed the slingshot from his waist, put the marble in the slingshot, and aimed it at Pickah's knees.

Pickah took a step back and started to smile nervously, revealing a mouth full of nicotine-stained and rotted teeth. "Lanky, careful wid dhat, mine you shoot . . ."

An approaching car drowned out Pickah's word. The cokehead looked at the approaching car, and his face was instantly transformed into a fearful mask. He dropped the black plastic bag he had in his hand and sprinted off toward an eight-foot wall that separated the housing scheme from a patch of open land. When he got to the wall, he jumped and reached with his two hands for the top of the wall. With both hands on the wall, he sprang over it and disappeared from Lanky Roy's view.

The crunching of gravel beneath the spinning rubber drew Lanky Roy's attention back to the approaching car. He watched as it drove up and stopped a few feet from him. It was the same black BMW motorcar that had been parked on the roadside above the river earlier that day. Lanky Roy realized that the car belonged to Speng Shell, the area don. Lanky Roy has never spoken to Speng Shell before. Still, he would normally see the area leader at a few community peace parties or when the Member of Parliament visited the area.

Speng Shell was infamous for his crazy ways of keeping the peace in the community. He was both feared and respected by the residents of Iron Bridge and throughout the parish of Saint Catherine. He made his living mostly from extorting business people in the community. He also operated an illegal scrap metal business in a secluded part of the community.

The driver's door of the car opened, and a male teenage thug stepped out and walked up to Lanky Roy. He had on a pair of dark glasses and had a bright-red handkerchief wrapped around his head. He also had on a brand-new pair of white sneakers. His XX orange T-shirt was out of his pants, and there was a slight bulge on his right hip. Lanky Roy suspected the thug was one of Speng Shell's henchmen. The thug offered no greeting as he walked up to Lanky Roy and stopped in front of him.

"Yow," said the thug. An upper front row of shiny gold teeth glittered in his mouth. "The big man need to talk to you now."

Lanky Roy wondered what could the area don need to speak with him about. It could be either of two things, he thought: it could be either good or bad. He hoped it was not the latter. He had heard rumors of men's bones being broken because they had done or said something that offended Speng Shell; furthermore, there wasn't a part on Lanky Roy's ultra slim body that could take a good blow. Knowing that he has never done or said anything to offend the area leader, Lanky Roy mustered a little courage and walked toward the car.

The gold-toothed thug stopped Lanky Roy by blocking the skinny young man with his body. "No," he said, pointing to the gate. "Open you gate, the big man want to park in you yard."

Lanky Roy was perplexed by the strange request, but he knew better than to protest. He took out the marble from the slingshot and put it back in his pants pocket, then pushed the slingshot in the waist of his pants. He thought about retrieving the screwdriver that he had put on top of the car's hood, but he decided against it. Gold Teeth was watching him too closely, so he turned around and walked to the gate. He opened both sides of the gate in order to al-low the car to drive through. The rusty hinges on the gate made a loud creaking noise as if it didn't like the idea of having any suspicious characters enter. A second thug, who was also wearing sunglasses, got out from the front passenger seat of the car and walked to the gate. He looked at Lanky Roy with a dead-serious look on his face. There were several wrinkles in the middle of his forehead; it was as if he had never smiled since he was born.

The gold-toothed thug got back into the huge car and reversed it through the gate. He parked beneath the mango tree, close to the doghouse. He left the engine running and stepped out of the car. He opened the right back passenger door and indicated with a big finger to Lanky Roy that he should go in.

Lanky Roy looked toward the gate. The dead-serious-looking thug had closed the gate and was standing guard in front of it. Lanky Roy silently prayed that Peaches's friend had scratched or broken the DVD so that Peaches would stay and argue about it. He knew that would keep her from coming home anytime soon. He didn't want anything to happen to her and Baby Tiffany, and he also didn't want her to see him in a situation in which he had no control in his own yard. A bruised ego would be an understatement. Inevitably, he looked at Putus for some sort of protection, but he got none. The huge Rottweiler was fast asleep as usual. Lanky Roy was about to step in the car when Gold Teeth stretched out a hand to him.

"Gimme," said Gold Teeth.

"Give you what?"

"The slingshot."

Lanky Roy wanted to ask the thug if he was really serious, but he didn't bother. He removed the slingshot from his waist and handed it over to Gold Teeth, who took it and tossed it in Putus's direction. The slingshot landed beside Putus's head, but the dog was too busy sleeping to notice. Lanky Roy shook his head and stepped in the car.

Gold Teeth wound down Lanky Roy's window fully so he could see inside. He closed the door and stepped back a few feet from the car, facing the open window.

*   *   *

Perching on an electrical wire across the road from Lanky Roy's gate was Kas Kas, the pigeon that was known for her notorious lying and news-carrying ways. Ever since Mongrel had gotten away, the gray-and-white- feathered bird had been watching Lanky Roy's yard. She wanted to see what Lanky Roy would do to the mongrel dog if he came back. She wanted to be the first one to spread the news.

The moment Kas Kas saw the human area leader and his two thug disciples come to visit Lanky Roy, she suspected something fishy. Eager to find out was going on, she flew off the electrical wire and landed on top of Putus's doghouse. The closer to the action, the juicier the news—that was Kas Kas's philosophy.

Gold Teeth admired the friendly-looking pigeon that had landed close by him and smiled at it. If he only knew who Kas Kas was.

*   *   *

In the backseat of the car, Lanky Roy looked at Speng Shell, who was sporting a clean, bald head. Lanky Roy could almost see his reflection on the area don's shiny black scalp. Speng Shell was dressed in black jeans and a black long-sleeved shirt. All the buttons on the front of the shirt were open. A white undershirt he had on contrasted against his black outfit. Around his neck, he wore a thin gold chain with a real .357 magnum spent shell as a pendant. It was rumored that the spent shell was taken from the body of the first person he killed. He also had a small spliff in the corner of his mouth. He removed the spliff from his mouth and flicked it with accuracy through Lanky Roy's open window. He looked at Lanky Roy with two piercing eyes and spoke with a smooth voice. "The soon-to-be-famous Lanky Roy," he said, "thanks to attend this unexpected meeting." He removed a chocolate bar from his shirt pocket, unwrapped it, and took a large bite.

"A don't have a choice, big man," said Lanky Roy. "And what fame you talking about?"

Speng Shell looked at him with a smirk on his face. "A sure you going make the evening news tonight." He pointed the chocolate bar at Lanky Roy. "Cause it was you who star the show at the riverside today."

Lanky Roy felt a wave of relief rush through his entire body. He was glad Speng Shell was not there to tell him that he had "dis-the-order"—a term the area don used when he thought someone in the community did something that they should be punished for. "Well, a never really trying to star a show," said Lanky Roy, leaning back in the car seat.

"Really?"

"Yeah, a was just trying to protect the community from that croc," Lanky Roy explained. "And get rid of a old mongrel dog at the same time—you know, kill two bird with one stone."

Speng Shell nodded. "A admire you bravery. Which bring us to the purpose of this meeting."

"Boss, no offense, but what a tired mongrel dog and a stray crocodile have to do with this meeting?" asked Lanky Roy, looking a bit confused. "Is not like a capture a rapist or a shop thief who did a terrorize the community."

Speng Shell took another bite from his chocolate bar and looked at Lanky Roy. "No, but you was the only one at the river who have the heart to throw the mongrel dog to the croc."

"Throw the mongrel to the croc?" asked Lanky Roy. He did not get the area don's point. "When you say a brave, a believe you mean, brave to face the crocodile."

"Well, if that was the case, you big-mouth friend would be at this meeting," said Speng Shell, "because him faced the crocodile too."

Lanky Roy didn't understand what Speng Shell was trying to say. The area don was toying with him, and he didn't have time for games. His rent was due in a week, and his girlfriend was giving him an attitude. He wished the area don would get to the point, but he was scared to tell him. "Boss, no offense, but a don't understand—"

"Lanky, what a saying is, Yabba or no one else at the riverside never have the heart to fling a live dog to the crocodile." The area don waited to see how the lanky man sitting beside him would react to his compliment.

Lanky Roy looked through his open window at the gold-toothed thug who was looking up in the mango tree. "A was just simply doing the community a favor," he said.

A creepy smiled appeared on Speng Shell's face. "Nice, now a want you to do the community a even greater favor."

Lanky Roy looked at the area leader. "Greater favor?"

"Yeah," said Speng Shell. "Independence Day is next Friday, the Member of Parliament have big tings plan for his constituency. A get the job to see that the community is properly clean up before him visit." He took the last bite of the chocolate and crushed the empty wrapper into a ball in the palm of his hand.

Lanky Roy started to like where the meeting was going. *Probly Peaches could get a job in the clean-up project and work some money for herself, and mi could work some money to pay the rent and buy a battery for the car,* he thought.

"You hear what a just say?" asked Speng Shell, interrupting Lanky Roy's thoughts.

"Yeah, man . . . yeah. A hear the MP want all the town square and housing scheme in him constituency to be the cleanest on the island."

The area don nodded. "Yeah, that is the objective."

"Okay, nice," said Lanky Roy. He was still thinking about employment for Peaches. "The man them can cut the grass, and all the woman them can sweep the garbage—"

"Not this kinda garbage," said Speng Shell, showing the crushed chocolate wrapper to Lanky Roy. He tossed the crushed wrapper through Lanky Roy's open window without taking his eyes off the lanky man.

Lanky Roy was confused by what Speng Shell had said to him. He thought the cleanup process would entail picking up scraps of paper off the ground and cutting grass, but the sweet-toothed area don was saying it wasn't about that. "What you mean the garbage is not like what you just dash through the window?" he asked.

"The garbage am talking is the four-legged kind that is running all over the place," said Speng Shell, watching Lanky Roy's reaction. "Especially all the mangy dogs in the area."

Lanky Roy scratched the right side of his head. "You going to get rid a all the mangy dogs in the community?"

"Not mi, you. A willing to pay you to do it, and not just the mangy dogs, all stray and sick animals that is a sore eye to the community."

"All a them?" asked Lanky Roy.

"Yes, everyone. A want them all disappear before Independence Day."

Lanky Roy sighed and scratched the right side of his head again. "Yeah, but why—"

"Listen," said Speng Shell. He removed a red handkerchief from one of his back pants pockets and began to wipe his hands and mouth. "The last time the MP come down here and give a speech, him step in dog crap. Him have to throw away him shoes and walk to him car in him socks alone."

Well, Lanky Roy thought, *considering that the last time the MP come down here, him was talking pure crap, it did suit him good to step in some.* Lanky Roy never dared voice his opinion out loud to Speng Shell; he didn't want to end up on the cleanup list.

*   *   *

On top of the doghouse outside, Kas Kas couldn't hear or see what was happening in the car. She flew off the doghouse and landed onto a limb of the mango tree that was hanging directly over the car. She wanted to see if she could look through the sunroof of the car, but the sunroof wasn't open. Kas Kas was determined to find out what was going on. Come hell or high water; she was going to leave that yard with some news. She looked down and saw the ugly-looking, gold-toothed human looking up in the tree at her. She didn't like him one bit. She returned her focus at the black car while she waited patiently on the limb of the tree.

*   *   *

Inside the car, Lanky Roy was scratching the right side of his head even harder as he listened to Speng Shell explaining why he had to get rid of all the stray and sick-looking animals in the community. "Is part of a beautification project," said Speng Shell, returning the handkerchief to his pants' back pocket. "A community cannot look good if it full a mangy dog, stray goat, and lame fowls running and crapping all over it. Them have to get rid of."

Lanky Roy nodded. "A get you point, boss, but who else know about this?"

"Only mi, you, and mi bwoys them outside," said Speng Shell. "The MP hire mi to clean up the community. Him don't know my method."

Lanky Roy was pleased to hear that. "Okay. So how much cheese you willing to pay mi for this job?"

Speng Shell gave Lanky Roy a wide smile, showing two rows of ivory-looking white teeth. "Ahh, now we talking business. Five grand per dog, three grand per goat, two grand per puss, and a grand for each fowl."

Lanky Roy's eyes sparkled as he began to fantasize about the potential of making big bucks. *If a pull off this job, it would solve mi money problem. Baby Tiffy would never run out of diaper again,* he thought. "But, boss, how a going catch all a them animals?"

"It easy, Lanky," said Speng Shell. "For the puss, set a cage with some butter at night. A puss cannot resist butter. Just move them and the cage before morning."

Lanky Roy asked, "Where a going get cage, boss?"

"Don't worry, them is at a welder shop ready to pick up," said Speng Shell. "Now, if a animal is sick, it shouldn't hard to catch, just pick it up and hide it until you ready to move all the others."

Lanky Roy started to realize that the job wasn't going to be an easy one. "And the fowl them, boss. Fowl can fly, you know. If you never notice, them have two wing. Them no easy to catch."

"That easy, Lanky," said Speng Shell, leaning back in his seat. "Fowls love corn grain. All you have to do is soak some corn grain in some rum and throw it, give them. In less than five minutes, them drunk."

Lanky Roy made a slight chuckle. "A never think of that. But, boss, where mi going keep all a them animals?"

The area don pointed toward the gate. "Put them in you car. Is a station wagon, it big enough. It look like it can hold the entire Old MacDonald farm."

"Okay, boss, but what about the dogs them?"

"What you mean?" asked Speng Shell.

"A mean, how mi a going catch them? Mi can't just grab them with mi bare hand. Them a mongrel, and mongrel dog bite hot."

"The same thing you going do for the stray goats, a the same you going do for the stray dogs," said Speng Shell.

Lanky Roy waited in suspense. He wanted to hear what other options he could use to dispose of Mongrel just in case the runaway dog came back to the yard. Speng Shell seemed to have that option.

"For the dogs and goats, you going to use these," said Speng Shell. He pulled out a black plastic bag from beneath the back of the front passenger seat. From the plastic bag, he removed a huge bunch of tranquilizer darts that were held together by a large rubber band. Each of the darts was about four inches in length. There was a small plastic cap at the small end of each dart. A red tuft with fibrous-looking material was attached at the thick end of each dart to guide the dart toward its target.

Speng Shell spun the dart around with the tip of his big and index fingers. "A buy these from a friend who work at a vet clinic in Kingston. Them already full a tranquilizer. All you have to do is pull off the cap." He removed the small plastic cap, exposing a shiny half-inch needle.

Lanky Roy looked at the dart in Speng Shell's hand. "Boss, so where is the dart gun, them tings here normally come with a gun, right?"

"The gun is too long, it hard to conceal," said the area don. "Is not like you going approach any aggressive animal. All you have to do is walk up to the dog or goat, aim, and throw it like you playing a game a dart. Just make sure you throw it hard."

Lanky Roy took the dart from Speng Shell's hand and examined it. He looked at the rest of the darts that Speng Shell had in his other hand. "Is about three dozen darts you have, what a must do with the leftovers?"

The area don threw the bunch of darts on Lanky Roy's lap. "That is call incriminating evidence. Burn the leftovers. A will send somebody to pick up the cage when you finish with them."

Lanky Roy smiled while he thought about having fun with the darts. He lifted the dart in his hand and mimed a throw toward the car's front windshield. "A can't wait to use them dart here."

"Now," said Speng Shell.

Lanky Roy looked at the area don. "What you just say?"

"You say you can't wait to use the darts, so a say, you going get to use it now."

Lanky Roy was baffled by what Speng Shell had said to him. "Now, you want mi to start the job now?"

"No, you not going start capture the animals them till tomorrow night," said Speng Shell, looking amused. "But you going start practice to use the darts right now."

"Practice now, on what?

Speng Shell leaned close to Lanky Roy and gave him one of the most deadly smiles Lanky Roy had ever seen. "That lovely Rottweiler dog you have outside."

Lanky Roy was shocked to his core. His blood ran cold; it was as if his heart had suddenly started to pump ice-cold water through his veins. "What . . . you . . . want mi to use the dart on mi expensive dog, boss?"

"Relax, Lanky, let mi ask you a question. You have cable?"

Lanky Roy didn't understand how cable TV came in the equation, but he decided to answer. "Yes," he said.

"You ever watch any type a documentary where them training police?"

Lanky Roy was even more confused. "Ye-yeah," he said.

"Good, you notice that them spray pepper spray in the trainee's them eyes, sometime even tase real police officers with a Taser gun?"

Lanky Roy nodded and swallowed a huge lump of bile.

"You know why them do that?" asked Speng Shell.

"No," said Lanky Roy, silently wishing he could disappear through the roof of the car.

Speng Shell leaned closer to Lanky Roy and looked him in the eyes. "They do that so the trainees and police officers can feel and experience what them is going to do to the bad bwoys on the street."

It took Lanky Roy less than a second to realize what the area don was saying. "So you want mi to . . . to . . ." he stammered. He couldn't find his words; they were too frightening to say.

"Exactly, a want you to experience what them animal is going to feel," said Speng Shell, leaning back in his seat. "You lucky a never tell you to stick youself on you ass with the dart."

Perspiration started to run down Lanky Roy's temples. He could feel his shirt clinging to the small of his back. Even his toes had started to sweat in the old pair of Adidas sneakers he had on. "But, boss, a never my idea to . . . to throw the mongrel dog in the river, it was the big-mouth bwoy Yabba."

Speng Shell shook his head. "Yes, but it was you who volunteer to throw the mongrel in the river. It was you who volunteer to put the bell around the cat—"

"Bell, which bell, which cat?" asked Lanky Roy. He scooted in his seat closer to his door.

"Is a figure a speech, idiot. Look, you already agree to do the job, you can't back out," said Speng Shell. He pointed toward Lanky Roy's door. "Now, step out a the car and put that pet dog of yours to a temporary sleep."

"But, boss, him already asleep, from a buy him, him don't stop sleep."

"Well, put him into a deeper sleep."

Lanky Roy picked up the bunch of darts out of his lap, opened the door, and stepped out of the car. *What the hell a get into,* he wondered.

Outside the car, Lanky Roy looked around to see if anybody else other than Speng Shell and his two thugs were watching him. Gold Teeth was examining a young mango in his hand that had fallen from the tree. At the front of the gate, Dead Serious was smoking a cigarette. Lanky Roy heard the other back door of the car open. He turned to see Speng Shell getting out of the car.

The area don walked around and leaned on the back of the car. He folded his arms and began to watch Lanky Roy like a hawk.

*   *   *

Up in the mango tree, Kas Kas spotted the dart in Lanky Roy's hand and realized that this was what she had been waiting for. She didn't know what was about to take place, but whatever it was, it looked like it was certainly newsworthy. She gripped the tree branch with her two claws firmly and waited for what was to come.

*   *   *

With the bunch of darts in his left hand, Lanky Roy looked at the single dart in his right hand. He looked at Putus, who was still sleeping. He took a small step to the sleeping animal, just as the huge dog opened its eyes, lifted up its head, and looked at him.

"Blow wow, Putus, of all the time, a now you choose to wake up?" Lanky Roy grumbled to himself.

Putus stood up, stretched his legs, and wagged his tail at his master. Lanky Roy looked at Speng Shell, who gave him the go-ahead nod with his head. Lanky Roy hesitated, and Gold Teeth walked up to him with an intimidating look on his face. Lanky Roy quickly turned his attention back to Putus. He walked to the dog, lifted his hand with the dart, and aimed it at the animal.

To everyone's surprise, Putus lifted one of his back legs toward the trunk of the mango tree as if he was about to pee. Lanky Roy lowered his arm with the dart and looked at Speng Shell.

"Don't wait until him finish pee pee," said Speng Shell.

Lanky Roy shook his head and stepped back.

Gold Teeth started to massage the bulge on his right hip while looking at

Lanky Roy. He also moved closer to get a good look at the four-legged target. Lanky Roy stepped closer to Putus and raised his arm with the dart. He pulled back his arm and thrust the dart forward in the air just as Putus began to spray the trunk of the mango tree with pee.

The dart glided through the air and landed on Putus's left rump. The huge dog gave out a slight yelp as his four knees began to collapse beneath him. He slowly sat on the ground and then lay on his right side. Like an out-of-control water hose, the dog's penis shot pee toward Lanky Roy and Gold Teeth. A huge splash of pee landed all over Gold Teeth's ankle and pair of white sneakers. He jumped back and hopped all over as he tried to flash off the hot dog pee that was running down the inside of one of his shoes. He quickly took off the dog-peed shoe while cursing.

Lanky Roy wanted to laugh, but he feared that if he did, Gold Teeth would not only massage his right hip but also pull out whatever was causing the bulge. He looked at Putus, who was still lying on the ground. The peeing had stopped, but the dog's eyelids were closing. In less than two minutes, Putus was knocked out cold.

Lanky Roy looked at the tranquilized dog lying on the ground. *If a can do this to mi expensive dog, then a can do it to any stray animals in the area,* he said in his mind. The sound of a single applause broke him out of his thoughts. He turned to see Speng Shell clapping his hands and walking over to him.

"Good, Lanky, good," said Speng Shell. "See, it easy. You pass you audition because you brave."

Lanky Roy looked at Putus and scratched the right side of his head. "Yeah, but—"

"Don't worry," said Speng Shell. He walked to Putus and removed the dart from the dog's rump. "Mi friend at the vet clinic said the sedative will last about ten minutes on a good-size dog."

"Oh, that no bad then," said Lanky Roy.

Speng Shell walked to Lanky Roy and handed him the dart. "Get rid a this."

"No prob, a going burn it," said Lanky Roy. He took the used dart from the area don and put it with the other unused darts.

There was a commotion at the gate. The three men looked toward the gate, where they saw Dead Serious blocking Peaches and Clifton from entering the yard.

"Let the lovely lady in her yard, man," said Speng Shell.

They all watched as Dead Serious released the latch on the gate and allowed Clifton and Peaches to pass. As she entered the yard with Baby Tiffany in her hand, Peaches looked at the small crowd and gave Lanky Roy a what-the-hell-is-going-on-here look. Clifton limped behind her with a pack of diapers and a bootleg DVD in his hand. Peaches was about to say something, but before she could utter a word, Lanky Roy pointed to the veranda. "The two a you go inside, a will explain everything to you later."

Peaches gave Speng Shell and Gold Teeth a dirty look and balanced Baby Tiffany with one hand while pulling Clifton close to her with the other. She pushed the veranda grille open and went into the house.

Speng Shell looked at Lanky Roy and smiled. "The real man a yard, that's how a woman must obey her man."

"Hmm," said Lanky Roy, looking at Putus, who was breathing a bit shallowly. "Boss, when a knocked out all the animals and put them in the car, what a must do with them?"

Speng Shell pulled out a black leather wallet from his pocket. "Don't worry," he said, removing five crispy one-thousand-dollar bills from the wallet. "All you have to do is drive the car behind the old train station. A truck will meet you there to transfer the animals to a dumping site."

Lanky Roy was happy to hear that he wasn't required to do the disposing of the animals. He asked the area leader where the truck driver was going to dump the animals.

Speng Shell gave him a suspicious look. "Why you want to know where the truck driver going dump them?"

"Just curious."

"Careful, Lanky, curiosity kill more than cat," said the area don. He looked at the skinny young man standing in front of him and wondered if he should divulge any more information to him. He figured he might as well tell him since the young man was already in too deep. "The truck driver will carry them to Ticks Island, a part of Saint Catherine. Miles of woodland, only crab, ticks, and biting insect live there."

"Rahtid, so far?" asked Lanky Roy.

"Far?" said Speng Shell. He handed the five one-thousand-dollar bills to Lanky Roy. "It could worst. A could carry them and dump them in a the bauxite red mud lake, where them would disappear forever."

"True," said Lanky Roy. "But, boss, what happen when the car get too full a the animals?"

"It won't get too full, Lanky. Every morning, the truck will meet you behind the old train station at five a'clock to pick up the animals that you catch the night before."

"So how much morning a going meet the truck?" asked Lanky Roy.

"When you put the last a the animals and fowls in you car, that's when you going make the last trip to the truck."

"Blow wow," said Lanky Roy scratching the right side of his head.

"What, you have a problem with that, Lanky Roy?"

"No no, boss, mi good," said Lanky Roy, looking at the money that Speng Shell had given him. "What this money for?"

"As a say before, five grand for a dog," said Speng Shell. He looked at Putus, who was still fast asleep. "A not saying you must get rid a you top dog, but am a man of mi word. Plus, encouragement sweetens the labor."

Lanky Roy pushed the money in his right front pants pocket. "Okay, boss, you can drop off the cage them anytime tomorrow."

"Yes, first ting in the morning," said Speng Shell. He walked to the left rear passenger door of the car and then stopped. He turned around to Lanky Roy. "Remember now, Lanky," he said, "all stray and sick animals must be missing by Independence Day. A will come an inspect the day before. Not even mosquito a don't want to see in a the area when a come."

"Don't worry, boss, all stray and sick animals will disappear by then."

"Good, glad you understand that," said Speng Shell. He turned and reached for the back passenger door handle. He was about to open the door when a splash of bird dropping fell on top of the car. He looked up in the mango tree, where he saw Kas Kas perching on a limb. "Yow, Lanky," he said, "Add pigeon to the list too. Same treatment as the fowl or use you slingshot."

"No problem." Lanky Roy laughed. He watched the area don get in the back of the car. Gold Teeth hopped into the driver seat with both shoes in his hand. Dead Serious opened the gate, and Gold Teeth drove the car out of the yard and stopped outside the gate. Dead Serious left the gate wide open and got in the front passenger seat of the car. The car sped off, leaving Lanky Roy looking at a cloud of dust.

Lanky Roy pushed his right hand in his right front pants pocket and felt the five thousand dollars against his fingers. He looked at the used dart among the bunch of unused darts in his left hand and took a deep breath. He walked toward the veranda, wondering how he was going to explain everything to his baby mother.

*   *   *

Up in the mango tree, Kas Kas couldn't move; she was paralyzed with fright. She had gotten more than she'd bargained for. The conversation between Speng Shell and Lanky Roy was so nerve-racking, it had caused her to empty her bowels. She didn't mean to poo on the area don's car, but nervousness had gotten a hold on her. "How can them humans so wicked and cruel?" she said. "Them planning on doing the most wicked act a ever hear about in mi entire bird life."

She decided she had to warn the other birds and animals in the area right away. She tried to fly, but her wings felt heavy. After a few attempts, she finally lifted off and flew in the direction of the cave. While she was flying, she wondered how she was going to convince the other animals and birds in the community that what she saw and overheard was true. *This going be one big task,* she thought as she flew away in the evening sky.

Chapter Eight

The sun slowly lowered itself in the west as a few birds flew toward the meeting at the cave. Mongrel had just cleared the graveyard and was walking through a cluster of trees. Dried twigs snapped beneath his feet as he walked. He was getting more tired and hungrier the more he walked. "Lord, a hungry," he said.

Out of the corner of one of his eyes, he saw a star apple tree. He stopped and admired the dozens of ripe, dark purplish fruits that were on the tree. Climbing wasn't one of Mongrel's fortes, so he knew to reach the fruits on the tree was impossible. He was about to walk away when he saw one of the tree's limbs on the ground. The limb looked as if it was torn from the tree by a strong wind. Like Christmas balls on an overturned Christmas tree, a few ripe star apples hung from branches on the torn limb. The skins of the fruits were a bit shriveled as if the limb was torn from the tree the day before.

Mongrel did not care about the looks of the fruit; he was too hungry to be choosy. He used his right front paw and knocked off one of the fruits from its stem. It fell to the ground, and Mongrel bit into the soft, fleshy fruit. Even though he was starving, he ate with caution. He didn't want to swallow any of the huge oval-looking black seeds inside the fruit. He had known a few dogs in the community who had accidentally swallowed a few of the seeds in the past and were constipated for days. He cautiously ravaged the inside of the fruit as its sweet milky juice ran down the corners of his mouth. After eating half a dozen of the fruit, Mongrel regained some energy. He licked his lips and resumed the journey to the cave, anticipating the excitement waiting there for him.

Chapter Nine

The grayish-white cave sat close to the base of a small hill less than a quarter of a mile from the graveyard and Fruit Basket. The cave was formed with two vertical limestone rocks that jutted out of the side of the hill. The rock formations were joined at the top, giving the front of the cave a triangular shape. A dark hollow opening lay between the rocks. The opening was about six feet tall and seven feet wide. Several trees, both tall and short, surrounded the cave. Some of the trees were armed with spiky thorns. The cave's existence had been around for hundreds of years and had served as a hideout for a few human runaway slaves back in the days of slavery on the island. The Animal Committee had started to use it as a secret meeting place in the early 1980s when it was alleged that a male human was killing stray dogs and putting their meat in soup.

It was alleged that the male human would sell the dog soup in Cross Roads, a popular shopping neighborhood in Kingston. A famous mongrel dog named Rebel Bone—who was the founder and first president of the Iron Bridge Animal Committee—had started to recruit animals in the community to fight against the dog soup crisis. No one had ever actually caught the soup vender killing a dog, but quite a few mongrel dogs were missing from their homes and off the street during that time. Several dog skulls were also found in a gully in Kingston, so Rebel Bone didn't take any chances. An old male dog had suggested the uninhabited cave to Rebel Bone, who started to use it as the committee's headquarters.

Even after the death of Rebel Bone in 1994, the cave was still used for the committee's headquarters. There were a few humans who knew about the cave, but the few who visited it in the past never dared to return. For the animals, birds, and insects in the community, protecting the cave from human invasion was tantamount to protecting the prime minister at the Jamaica House. Dozens of grass lice were on every blade of grass and tree leaf in the area. Some of the most vicious and deadliest paper wasps on the island were positioned around the cave's perimeter. Their huge nests were also displayed at the entrance of the cave as a warning to the humans. There were also large red ants living outside the cave in old tree barks. They would normally help the wasps attack a human who was trespassing when it was necessary.

The humans had dubbed the cave as the John Crow Cave because Billy G had suggested that having a few John Crows perched on the top of the cave during the daytime would be a huge turn off for any humans on the island. No human on the island wanted to visit an area where groups of vultures congregated.

The outside of the cave was buzzing with most of the animals and birds in the community. Birds from all over Saint Catherine, Kingston, and Saint Andrew were there. Even a pair of Greater Antillean grackle—known on the island as a Kling Kling blackbird—was there for the meeting. The pair of birds was visiting from the parish of Manchester. There were lots of other birds. Some of them were perched on trees that were close to the cave. Some were talking while some were eating various seeds and corn grains that were laid out on the ground. The grains were on large green banana leaves that were provided by the Animal Committee.

A large congress of John Crows was hanging out on top of the cave. A few of them were perched on a tall coconut tree at the back of the cave that also served as a lookout post.

Three menacing mongrel dogs that called themselves the Hungry Belly Crew were standing under a nearby tamarind tree. They were all wondering what had become of Mongrel after he had escaped death.

A few feet from the dogs were two teenage male goats. They were each eating a sour orange while admiring a mother goat that was suckling her two kids across from them.

Hebrew, the humble and kind female donkey, was lying under a nearby guinep tree, munching on a root of guinea hen weed. Her coat was light gray, and the bones of her rib cages were showing at her two sides. Her skinny body was in contrast to the rest of the animals at the cave. It was known in the community that she had a long list of ailments, including arthritis of the knee. She was also blind in her left eye. She was blinded when her former master hit her with his whip when she could no longer pull his cart to the market one morning.

While Hebrew was snacking on the guinea hen weed, she was talking to Jacko, the spider, and the rest of his group. They had reached the cave a few minutes before and were resting under the guinep tree.

Jenny, the miserable common fowl, was also among them as well. After the bees had attacked Yabba and the rest of the humans, Jenny had sneaked out from beneath the tree trunk and headed for the cave. On her way to the cave, she met Hebrew, who offered her a piggyback ride. When they arrived, they saw Jacko and his group waiting for the meeting to start, so they both decided to hang out with them.

Nanny Stush, who was sitting beside Bruck Kitchen, looked around at everyone. She had noticed that none of the animals wanted to ask Hebrew about her human-cow-thief experience. She decided to brave it and mentioned the delicate subject. "I can't believe you survived that horrible experience, Ms. Hebrew."

Hebrew let out a slight chuckle and looked at Nanny Stush. "You survive yours today, so a guess Jesus is watching over the two a us."

"You're so right. What really happen?" asked Nanny Stush.

Jacko drew closer to Hebrew; he was salivating to hear the full story from her. All the others—except Guana, who was dozing off on the bunch of ripe banana—gave Hebrew their undivided attention.

"Well," said Hebrew, turning to Nanny Stush. "What happen, Ms. Nanny is—"

"Call me Nanny."

"Okay, Nanny," said Hebrew, "you see, am a Christian and a love to do good. Last Sunday night, a was at the riverside drinking when a see a little goat kid—"

"Goat kid?" asked Jacko.

"Yes," said Hebrew, giving Jacko a weird look. She didn't like to be interrupted. "The goat kid looked lost, so a ask him where him live and he told mi Pigeon Valley."

"That far bad," said Bruck Kitchen.

"Yes, very far," said Hebrew. "So a follow him home. That was about 8:00 p.m. By the time a was halfway home, it was about 8:30 p.m."

"Wow, that's late," Nanny Stush said.

Hebrew nodded. "That is true, so a decide to use Farmer Brown banana field as a shortcut."

Grunty shifted his weight on the ground. "Wrong move, Hebrew, you should stay on the main path."

"Yes, a should," said Hebrew. "That was when a accidentally run into the two human cow thief. They start to run after mi. They both have a cutlass."

"Oh my god, two machetes?" asked Nanny Stush.

"Yes, a never stop run until a reach mi yard," said Hebrew.

Jacko looked at Hebrew's four feet. "Then, is how you manage to run with them four arthritis knees, darling?"

Hebrew looked at her spider friend. "Well, Jacko, it is a different thing when you running for you life than when you running for fun."

"You right," said Jacko, "because it sound like Seabiscuit, the famous racehorse, would have a hard time catching up with you that night."

Guana, the green lizard, opened his eyes, yawned, and turned to Hebrew. "The next morning, a hear that them find you head, four foot, and tripe in Farmer Brown banana field."

"A bet you is Kas Kas start that rumor," said Jenny. She turned to Guana. "A thought you was sleeping."

Guana rubbed his eyes. "A was, but a wake up now. Yes, is Kas Kas start the rumor."

"That gyal Kas Kas getting out a hand with her lying," said Jacko. "And a can bet, you believe this rumor like how you believe the mongrel-missing-back-foot rumor, Guana."

"Yes, she catch mi twice to rahtid," said Guana. He turned to Hebrew. "A sorry you have to go through that with you sick knees, Hebrew."

Nanny Stush looked at Hebrew's skinny legs and sighed deeply. "I can't believe you had to go through that, and you're not well. These kinds of cruelty being inflicted on us animals by these cruel humans have to stop."

"True word," said Bruck Kitchen.

Jenny looked toward the entrance of the cave. "Them need to hurry up and start the meeting. A don't come here to waste time, a hope them know that."

Jacko broke off a finger of banana from the bunch of ripe bananas and looked at Jenny. "This is Jamaica, Jenny, nothing never start on time."

"Them need to sort out them thing because night coming," said Jenny. "I don't sure if when I reach a my roost tonight, a human won't in the tree lay waiting mi."

At that very moment, Mouth-a-Massi, the public announcement parrot, flew from out of the cave and landed in a sour orange tree that was close to the cave. He cleared his throat and began to address the animals and birds. "Everybody, listen up, the meeting going start in about five minutes, Billy G apologize for the delay. Again, the meeting will—"

"Aright, Mouth Almighty, we hear you, rest you beak, man!" shouted Gramps, an old one-legged rooster who was munching on a few corn grains by the banana leaves. The old rooster had black, orange, and red feathers. He had lost his left leg to a bird trap a few years before. He always found it a pleasure to tease Mouth-a-Massi whenever he got a chance.

Some of the animals and birds laughed at Mouth-a-Massi. The parrot ignored them and flew over to the pair of visiting Kling Kling blackbirds that were talking to some other birds. Mouth-a-Massi said something to the visiting birds then ushered them toward the cave.

No-Shame—the John Crow who was always fighting with War Plane, the pechary bird—watched from the tall coconut tree as Mouth-a-Massi guided the blackbirds in the cave. "Yes, man, is because them a visitors why them can go in before we!" he yelled.

"Shut you mouth, you must be nice to strangers!" shouted War Plane, who was talking to a turtle dove in the top of the guinep tree. "Only a John Crow would make a comment like that!" he continued.

"And only a inquisitive pechary chat so much," said No-Shame. "Mind you own business!"

War Plane flew out of the guinep tree and flew toward No-Shame.

No-Shame flew out of the coconut tree and tried to fly away from War Plane, but the angry bird chased him and pecked a few feathers out of his back.

All the animals and birds laughed as they watched No-Shame trying to escape War Plane's pecking beak. The laughing came to a sudden stop when someone called out Mongrel's name. They all turned and saw the mongrel dog walking slowly toward the cave.

Gramps hopped on his one leg to meet Mongrel. "Come in, star bwoy!" he shouted.

One of the kids got up from its mother's side and ran behind Gramps. The mother goat ran after the kid and carried it and the other kid into the cave.

All the birds flew on the ground beside Mongrel. All the animals, along with Jacko and his group, walked over to greet the mongrel dog as well. Some of them began to examine his body for bruises and scratches. Hebrew gave him a sympathetic pat on the back. Like reporters quizzing a celebrity, they all started to ask him questions simultaneously; questions were being fired at him from all angles.

"What it feel like to be so near the croc?" asked Grunty.

"Did him teeth scrape you?" asked Cutter, a large male rat.

"Did any of the big stone that the humans throw at you catch you?" asked Jenny

"How you—"

"Hey, Mongrel!" shouted No-Shame from the top of the coconut tree. "How much teeth the crocodile have?"

"Ignore that idiot, Mongrel," said Gramps. "At least you not missing one foot like mi." He laughed.

Jacko turned to Guana, who had climbed on a nearby tree limb. "Guana, look for youself. Is lie Kas Kas telling, Mongrel four foot intact."

"A not believing notting that she tell mi again," said Guana.

Hebrew asked, "Is now you learning that, Guana?"

A few of the animals and birds laughed at Guana. The green lizard looked away embarrassingly and hid his face with a tree leaf.

Mouth-a-Massi flew out of the cave and hovered over the crowd. "Everybody, listen up, the cave is ready. Billy G apologize for the delay."

"Whatever," said Jenny, "look how long we out here waiting?"

Most of the animals and birds rushed to the cave's entrance while pushing and shoving. None of them could get inside because of the huge traffic jam they caused. Jacko and his group stood back and watched as the pushing and shoving grew more intense.

A large group of security wasps rose from one of the big nests that were close to the cave's entrance. They launched in the air and circled the unruly crowd. Some of them flew to the entrance of the cave and blocked it with their bodies. The pushing crowd pulled back as the security wasps flew all around them.

Stinger, the leader of the wasps, flew from his position at the very entrance of the cave and faced the crowd. "Yow yow," he said, "what kind of behavior this? You all a carry on like some human hooligans!"

Gramps, the one-legged rooster, hopped out of the way of several stamping feet. "A true, man, is like them want crush mi one good foot to rahtid."

Stinger advanced to the crowd with his large bright orange wings beating rapidly. "Yow, a want one line. We have visitors here, and look how you all a carry on."

They all started to calm down and formed one line. Stinger did not move until they were all settled down. After he was satisfied with their cooperation, he flew back to his position at the entrance of the cave. He signaled to the swarm of security wasp that was blocking the entrance to allow the crowd to go through. The security wasps all flew back to their nests at the entrance of the cave. All the birds and animals filed into the cave for one of the most important meetings ever to take place there.

CHAPTER TEN

The Member of Parliament's white seven-bedroom mansion located at Ridge Mount Acres—an affluent neighborhood that had several expensive houses overlooking Spanish Town, the capital of Saint Catherine—was a beauty of its own. One could see the huge white house with its red-tile roof from as far as five miles during the daytime, and admire the beauty of its exterior lights during the nights.

Like a long black snake, the winding road leading to the Ridge Mount neighborhood was meticulously asphalted to perfection. The four tires of Speng Shell's black BMW motorcar hugged the road as Gold Teeth took a sharp turn that led to the gate of the mansion. Gold Teeth slowed the car to a stop in front of a tall, white electrical sliding gate that had a six-foot concrete column at each end of it. Dead Serious exited from the front passenger side of the car and walked up to the right column. There was an outdoor security camera mounted on top of the column and an intercom attached to the front of it. He pushed a small round button on the intercom and waited for a response. While he waited, he lifted the front of his plain white T-shirt to his nose and sniffed it. He wanted to make sure that the shirt didn't smell of marijuana smoke. The last time they had come to the Member of Parliament's house, the MP told Speng Shell that he didn't like the scent of ganja in his house. The MP's complaint hadn't stopped the area don and his thugs from taking a quick smoke of the dried hemp plant before they arrived at the gate that day. Satisfied that the shirt had a normal scent to it, Dead Serious straightened the front of it with the palm of his hand and looked toward the car. The large black car looked like a chimney on wheels as marijuana smoke rose lazily from its sunroof.

The intercom speaker crackled as it came to life with a female's voice from within the huge house. "Good afternoon, kani help you?"

"Yes, tell the big man that Speng Shell here to see'm," said Dead Serious.

"There is no big man here, only the MP, and he wasn't big the last time a see him."

"Look here, lady, just tell the MP that Speng Shell here to see'm, an' cut the long argument."

"Hold on," said the female's voice. The intercom returned to a dead silence. The security camera that was mounted on top of the column started to rotate toward Dead Serious. It stopped and stayed on him for a few seconds, then swiveled and focused on the car for about a minute. After what seemed to be an eternity to Dead Serious, the tall gate began to slide to the right as it opened. Dead Serious stepped aside to allow the car to drive through. As soon as the gate was opened wide enough, Gold Teeth drove the car through and stopped a few feet from it. Dead Serious jumped into the front passenger seat of the car and slammed the door shut. Gold Teeth drove the car up an asphalted driveway that led to the house while the gate closed behind them slowly.

The surface of the driveway was smooth. It was cut between a well-manicured lawn that covered the entire property. More than two-dozen royal palm trees were planted on each side of the driveway. Most of the trees were about fifty feet tall and were planted about fifteen feet apart. Their long green leaves swayed in the evening breeze as the BMW continued toward the huge house.

* * *

The stylish two-story white house was nicely situated in the middle of the property. The building was burglar-bars free and had two huge verandas, an upper and a lower. A garage, with its large automatic door closed, was built in the lower left of the house. Painted in an almond color, the garage door contrasted sharply against the rest of the house. Two huge bodyguards, about six feet tall, entered through a white front door of the lower veranda and looked at the approaching car. They were both dressed in blue jeans and black T-shirts. The smaller of the two stayed at the patio door while the other, who had a thick neck the size of a coconut tree trunk, walked up to the car that had stopped close to the house.

The thick-necked bodyguard used a fat knuckle to knock on Gold Teeth's driver window. The noise from the bodyguard's knuckle pounded in Gold Teeth's right ear. He gave the bodyguard a mean stare and wound down all the windows of the car.

Thick Neck leaned over and began to scrutinize the occupants of the car. Inside the car, Dead Serious was spraying cologne onto his shirt from a small glass bottle. Thick Neck smiled at the thug's activity and then looked toward the backseat of the car, where Speng Shell was sitting. He acknowledged the area don with a nod and walked to the back of the car. The trunk of the car flew open, and he examined the interior of the trunk. He spoke into a mike that was attached to an earpiece in one of his ears. "All clear," he said.

The huge automatic garage door began to roll upward, revealing a long, black Lincoln motorcar. Gold Teeth drove the car into the enormous garage and parked parallel to the Lincoln. Gold Teeth and his passengers all got out of the car as the garage door closed behind them like a giant clam engulfing its prey.

An inner door in the garage leading to the inside of the house opened with a soft creak. Member of Parliament, the Honorable Patrick Mullings, a tall and slim brown-skinned man in his early sixties, stood in the door and watched as his visitors got out of the BMW. The MP was dressed in a blue V-neck T-shirt, blue shorts, and a pair of blue house slippers. The majority of his low-cut hair was gray, but a few small patches of black hair were still visible on the sides of his head. The Member of Parliament had been in politics ever since he graduated from the University of Michigan in the United States back in 1973. After earning a degree in political science at the university, he had returned to the island to pursue a career in politics. For the last four years, he had been the minister for the Ministry of Water, Land, Environment, and Climate Change for the ruling political party on the island. He was well- loved and respected by his constituency that he represented in parliament. Mullings turned to the second bodyguard from the patio that was lurking a few feet behind him. "It's okay, Philip," he said, "you can leave us."

Philip walked away, and Mullings motioned with a hand to Speng Shell and his cronies to follow him.

Speng Shell looked at Philip and then looked at the MP. "You need to tell them two bulldog bodyguard to cut out the searching thing when we come here, you know."

Mullings ignored the area don's comment and led him and his two thugs into the huge house. They entered an enormous living room that smelled of tropical air freshener. The living room was well furnished with lots of expensive furniture. Among the furnishing were a six-piece sofa and a massive entertainment center made from genuine mahogany. In the middle of the entertainment center was a huge ninety-two-inch flat-screen television. The gigantic television was turned on. On the screen, there was s swimsuit commercial showing. In the commercial, a female model with an ebony skin tone walked on one of the island's sandy white beaches, wearing a two-piece bathing suit. Gold Teeth stopped suddenly to feast his eyes on the model's long legs, causing Dead Serious to bump into him accidentally.

Dead Serious pushed Gold Teeth on his shoulder and whispered. "Walk up, man. First you see a woman in bathing suit?"

Gold put an index finger to his mouth. "Shhh, an stop the noise in the man house."

Mullings stopped and turned to see what was happening behind him. He looked at the two thugs, shook his head, and continued to walk.

The area don and his thugs exited the living room and followed the MP into a long hallway. Photos of various Jamaican government personnel, including the current governor-general and prime minister, lined the entire left wall of the hallway. Mullings walked to the end of the hall and stopped in front of a closed- door on his right. The MP pushed open the door, revealing a spacious office. The walls of the office were painted light orange. Mullings invited the men in and walked to a brown-leathered office chair that was behind a dark mahogany office desk. On top of the desk was a twenty-inch flat- screen video monitor. The monitor's screen was split in four quarters, showing colored images of the mansion's property, including the main gate. On top of the desk, there was also an office telephone and a four-by-six photo frame of a pretty little girl about six years of age. A white ceramic ashtray sat beside the photo frame on the desk. A thirty-inch flat screen monitor was attached to a wall that was facing the desk. The screen of the monitor was blank. A tall gray metal cabinet was in one corner of the room behind the desk.

The MP sat down in the office chair and watched as Speng Shell sat in a guest chair that was in front of the desk.

Gold Teeth and Dead Serious lingered behind Speng Shell's chair without taking their eyes off of the MP.

There was a soft knock at the door. Mullings looked at the door with a frown on his face. "Come on in," he said.

A fat, dark-skinned lady in her forties entered. She was dressed in a blue-and-white maid's uniform. She cleared her throat and gave her boss a polite smile before speaking. "Mr. Mullings, you want anything for you guest or youself, sir?"

"No thanks, Mertle. Serve the men what they want."

Mertle looked at Dead Serious and cut her eyes at him. She turned to Speng Shell. "Mr. Speng, what—"

"A okay, Ms. Mertle, thanks anyway," said Speng Shell. He looked at his two followers. "You two chill outside, mi and the MP have business to talk about."

Mullings opened his mouth as if he was going to say something to Speng Shell but then swallowed his words. He waited until Mertle and the two thugs exited the office before he spoke. "What the hell you think you doing, coming here unannounced like this?"

"Relax, Mullings—"

"Relax nothing," said the MP, getting up out of his chair. "You darn well know that the prime minister is talking about investigating politician and area dons connections."

"Hypocrites, every politician in Jamaica have a gunman on him payro—

"The last time we met here, a told you we couldn't meet here anymore," Mullings explained. "You can't be seen coming here, Speng Shell. Furthermore, my wife doesn't like the idea of you coming to our house."

Speng Shell shook his head and laughed. "Damn, Mullings, you just throw you wife under the bus. Anyway, mine you blood pressure. Order a drink a water from Mertle and cool yourself down."

"I'm not thirsty, and I'm serious—"

"Look, Mullings, you send message that you have something big in store for mi, and mi is not a man who love to wait in suspense."

"I would've arranged for us to meet at another location other than my home," said Mullings. He sighed and looked at the four-by-six photo of the little girl that was on the desk. "Listen, there is a lot going on now. My little granddaughter, Abigail, is in the hospital, recovering from an asthma attack."

"That don't sound good."

"She is not doing well," said the MP, sitting back down in his seat. "Furthermore, she is worried about her poodle that went missing yesterday morning."

The mention of a dog reminded Speng Shell of the mongrel dog at the riverside a few hours before. *It look like all dogs having a bad week,* he thought to himself. "Man best friend, eh?" he asked.

"Abigail and her poodle are the perfect examples of that phrase," said Mullings. "The darn dog just went missing like that yesterday morning."

"A see the reward sign all over the neighborhood when we was driving up," said Speng Shell, removing a chocolate bar from his top shirt pocket. "Fifty thousand dollar for a lost and found poodle, a would be jealous if a was a mongrel dog."

The MP stood up and walked to the file cabinet. "Yes, poodles are expensive dogs. Well, since you're already here, might as well get the suspense over with."

"I second that," said Speng Shell. He peeled away half of the chocolate wrapper and took a large bite.

Mullings pulled out the top drawer of the file cabinet and removed a rolled-up paper map and unfolded it. He walked back to the desk and laid it out on the desk in front of the area leader.

"This is ridiculous," said Mullings, smoothing out a wrinkle on the map's surface. "Can you believe those bodyguards of mine let a little poodle slip out of the house without them seeing it?"

Speng Shell swallowed a mouthful of chocolate. "A never know it was the poodle them was bodyguarding, a thought it was you. Anyway, a not interested how Mutt and Jeff mess up on them dog security. What the map for?"

Mullings tapped a finger on the map. "This map?"

"How much map in the room, boss?"

The MP ignored the insult and used a hand to rub his eyes. "Gosh, I need some good sleep. This is a map of—"

The ringing of the telephone on the desk cut off Mullings's voice. He held up a hand to Speng Shell and picked up the receiver. "Hello, oh hi, Dr. Otarie," he said. He listened to the person on the other end of the line. "Is she in the same state? Okay, good . . . She is asking for her dog?" Mullings looked at Speng Shell who was looking annoyed. "My wife will be there in a few," Mullings continued, "she left about twenty minutes ago, okay, goodbye, Doc."

Mullings hung up the phone and looked at Speng Shell. "Told you she's worried about her poodle, oh boy."

Speng Shell peeled back a layer of wrapping from his chocolate bar and looked at the MP. "Mullings, let mi tell you something," he said. "If one a my youth sick in the hospital and all him asking for is him pet dog, a leave him down there to make the dog take care of him. As a was saying, what the map for?"

The MP leaned over the map and ran a hand over it. "This is a map of the entire Iron Bridge area—community and all—goes all the way up to the hill with that cave."

Speng Shell looked at Mullings and cracked a smile. "Sound interesting, tell mi more."

"See all of this area?" said Mullings, circling the Fruit Basket and its surrounding area with his right index finger on the map. "All of these wastelands will be put to use soon. The government is going to build dozens of correctional centers, so that it can get most of them teenage troublemaking vagabonds off the streets."

Speng Shell took the last bite of his chocolate bar, crushed the empty chocolate bar wrapper in his hand, and looked Mullings dead in the eye. "So you know a have to be the foreman—or at least one a the foreman on this site?"

"Give me some credit," said Mullings. "Why do you think I said I have something big in store for you?" He opened a bottom drawer in the desk, removed a cigar from a box, and tapped it in the palm of his hand. "Listen, Speng, the government is investigating the illegal scrap metal situation across the island, so I know you have to stay low off that for now. So even though you don't know anything about construction, I have to find something else so you and your boys can have food in the meantime."

"Wise thinking," said Speng Shell. "Can't allow the thugs them to get hungry. When thugs hungry, them belly growl, and when thugs belly growl, them guns growl too."

"That's an understatement, and I need you and them for next year's general election," said Mullings. He lit the cigar and took a long puff.

"Well, as you know, Mullings, no Speng Shell, no winnings for you. Intimidation at the polling station is the oldest and most effective trick in the book."

Mullings sucked the cancerous smoke into his lungs before letting it out slowly between his lips. "I don't need a reminder that you're the best at that particular trick, Speng Shell."

"A have to make sure you don't get soft on mi," said the area don.

"I will never get soft, Speng Shell. I must regain my seat—whatever it takes to win. I can't afford to lose my constituency. It's a stronghold. That's why I want the entire constituency to look the best on Independence Day. You know, butter them up."

Speng Shell fanned the smoke from his nose. "True, but you don't even have to do that much," he said. "All you have to do during election time is give them a three grand and a white fowl, and you have them vote."

"Yes, I know," said the Member of Parliament. "These people don't vote for progress, they vote for a belly full. I'm planning to give them more than a one-day belly full. How's the cleaning up coming on?"

The area don smiled and threw the chocolate wrapper into a nearby trashcan. "Everything copacetic, you going proud how clean Johnson Lane and the surrounding area going be on Independence Day."

"Good, I love that. Listen, Speng, I will keep you posted on this correctional center project thing," said Mullings. He began to fold up the map. "The government is still deciding if they are going to touch the cave because it's not just a regular cave."

"They going build on the hill with the cave too?"

"You didn't see I pointed it out on the map a moment ago?"

"Listen, Mullings, mi is not a map person. A don't read map, a don't read blueprint, just tell—"

"Okay," said the MP, holding up a hand. "Yes, we are planning on building on the hill too, but the cave has historical nature. So some people in the opposition don't think we should build any kind of building structure near it."

"So what that mean?" asked Speng Shell.

Mullings sucked air through his teeth and exhaled sharply. "Um . . . that means, the correctional center project is going to be delayed, not much, just a little."

"Okay, a understand," said Speng Shell. "But you see, Mullings, a don't count my chickens before them hatch, so until this correction center thing come through, a going need some funds to keep the thugs them belly full."

The MP put the cigar in the ashtray that was on the desk and walked around to the front of the desk to the area don. "Speng, I can guarantee that it will come through. I even plan to announce it during my speech in the community on Independence Day, don't worry—"

"Funds, Mullings, funds. A don't give away surety for unsurety. A sure a the money you rob up in parliament, a don't sure a any correctional project—"

"Okay, okay," said the MP. He walked to the thirty-inch flat-screen monitor that was attached to the wall facing the desk. He held one of the top edges of the monitor and pulled the side that opened like the door on a microwave. The space on the wall where the back of the monitor was had exposed a small gray combination safe that was built into the wall. There was a single combination dial in the middle of the safe. Mullings used his body to block the area don's view and gently turned the combination dial a few times. The safe's door clicked open, and the MP removed a large bundle of five-thousand-dollar notes that was held together by two thick elastic bands. He closed the safe's door and pushed back the fake monitor against the wall. He then walked back to the desk and threw the bundle of money on top of it.

"This is two hundred thousand, let it last."

"Last?" asked Speng Shell. He grabbed the bundle of money off the desk and pointed it at the parliamentarian. "You, of all person, should know that nowadays, money don't have no value. A chicken feed money this."

"Okay, go now, leave," said Mullings. "You will hear from me before the Independence Day community speech about the correctional center project." He ushered the area don toward the door. "And please don't show up back at my house unannounced like this again. I am begging you, don't come back."

Speng Shell stopped at the door and turned facing the Member of Parliament. "A go anywhere a want to go, Mullings, a will stop come around when a feel like." He opened the door and walked away, leaving the MP standing there staring at him.

Mullings closed the office door, leaned against it, and took a deep breath. He regretted the day he got involved with the area don.

CHAPTER ELEVEN

Inside, the cave was spacious and comfortable. No bats, snails, or any other living thing was allowed to make the inside of the cave their home. The animals, insects, and birds had taken pride in keeping the inside of the cave immaculate. They had used the same kind of material that they used to make their nest and homes to cover the ceiling of the cave, which was lined with mud, sticks, leaves, and wood pulp. The strange interior decoration was not for beauty but for keeping any water from seeping through the natural cracks in the cave. A few small holes were purposely left open in the walls so air could come through and ventilate the inside of the cave. Several tall, transparent glass bottles were sitting on the floor of the cave. The bottles were positioned in the middle, the four corners, and at the front. The bottles were quart-sized, and they were the same kind of bottles that the humans used to sell their rum. The quart bottles were collected by some of the strong birds in the community, who lifted them from the local rubbish dump and flew them to the cave. Inside each of the bottles was about a dozen click beetles, known in the island as peenie wallie bugs. The peenie wallies gave off a yellow- greenish light from a pair of dorsal light organs. The clear glass bottles enhanced the light given off from the peenie wallies and illuminated the cave so that the animals and birds in the cave could see their way around.

All the animals were sitting on the floor, while the insects and lizards were on the walls. The birds were comfortably perched on two makeshift perches that were made out of long pieces of bamboo sticks that ran on the top of the cave from one wall to the next. Billy G, the president of the Animal Committee, had given the warning that no animal, insect, or bird was to urinate or defecate inside the cave. It was a warning that all the bats in the community despised; because of that, they tended to stay away from most of the meetings. All the animals below were particularly grateful for the no-defecating rule because they were sitting beneath the buttocks of all the birds who were perched above their heads.

Jenny, the miserable female common fowl, had decided to hang out with Hebrew and the rest of Jacko's group at the back of the cave. Jack Hammer, the woodpecker, was perched observing the crowd below him. The only other bird who was not on the perch was Mouth-a-Massi because he had excused himself to take a latrine break outside and had not gotten back inside since. They all had forgotten about Mouth-a-Massi and were talking about Mongrel's near-death experience at the riverside. They had even overlooked that Nanny Stush was attending the meeting for the first time. No other gossip or situation could upstage the Mongrel riverside drama.

The pair of Kling Kling blackbirds from Manchester was perched comfortably on the visitor's section. The visitor's section had a well-polished thin bamboo for visiting birds and a woven mat made out of coconut leaves for visiting animals. Both the perch and mat were located at the front of the crowd.

Sitting beside the pair of Kling Kling blackbirds on the visitor's perch was a red-billed streamertail bird, known in the island as a doctor bird. The small bird had glossy-looking green and black feathers and two streamer-like long black tails hanging from his body.

Next to the visitor's section—where the rest of the animal committee board members were—there was a female mule with a dark brown coat and a red-skinned Red Poll bull. The large, hornless bull looked on at the crowd as he chewed his cud with a contented look on his face. Four years ago, when he was a young calf, he had run away from a nearby cow farm because his master was planning to castrate him. He knew castration meant he was destined for the corned beef tin, so he ran away one night with his two testicles intact. Both he and the female mule were sitting and waiting for their turn to speak.

Billy G, the wise old billy goat, was at the very front of the crowd, giving a speech. The hair on his body was brown and black and had lost its sheen. He had a four-inch gray beard that grew below his chin. The old goat had been the president of the Animal Committee ever since the death of Rebel Bone. He tilted his head back to position the frame of a pair of reading glasses that was on his nose. The frame was made from wire, and both of the lenses were missing from it. Billy G had found it on the riverbank a few years ago and decided to wear it because he believed that the reading glasses frame gave him an image that fit his personality and seniority. "Gentle peeps," he said, "as you can see, today has been a very sad day for us. Lanky Roy is an evil human and has acted out of grievance toward Mongrel, our dear animal friend."

Some of the animals agreed with Billy G by nodding. A few of them looked at Mongrel and shook their heads out of sympathy.

"Wicked and evil," said Lorna, a pregnant mongrel dog.

"Thanks, Lorna," said Billy G. "I can only imagine how traumatizing it was for him and the others who almost fell victims themselves."

Mongrel, who was sitting beside Jacko and his group at the back of the cave, nodded in agreement. Billy G had suggested to Mongrel that he should sit up front, but Mongrel had gotten stage fright and decided to sit with Jacko and the others instead. The excitement was too much for him. "You is so right, Billy, a was really traumatize," he said.

Nanny Stush looked at Mongrel. "Traumatize is an understatement, my friend."

"You right, Nanny," said Jacko, turning to Mongrel. "Bwoy, Mongrel, a hear today at the riverside was like the 2008 Olympics."

"Olympics, what you mean?" asked Mongrel.

"A hear that when Lanky Roy dash you in the river the second time, you swim out a the water like Michael Phelps, and when you reach on the other side a river, you shot off like Usain Bolt."

Jenny, who was looking miserable as usual, turned to Hebrew. "Some of us don't take this thing serious," she said. "This is nothing to joke about. Billy G need to come up with a solution."

Bruck Kitchen said, "That is why him call the meeting, Jenny."

"Yes, Brucky," said Jenny, "but some people too immature, they take everything for a joke."

Jacko turned to Bruck Kitchen. "Is mi she throwing her words for, you know, Brucky."

"A throw mi corn, a never call any fowl," said Jenny.

"That sound very strange coming from a fowl, Jenny." Jacko laughed.

Jenny rose from the ground where she was sitting and stormed toward the front of the crowd. When she reached the very front of the crowd, she walked to Billy G and stopped in front of him.

"Hello, Ms. Jenny, you look upset, what's the matter?" asked Billy G. Even though he knew that was how Jenny looked all the time, he still wanted to find out.

"Billy G, a almost get kill today when a group a human chase mi down to catch mi to use mi as crocodile food—"

"I'm sorry, Ms. Jenny, before we leave here, I hope we all come up with a solution."

"Billy G, some people don't take it serious," said Jenny. "Today mi and Mongrel could end up dead. Can you imagine get eat alive by a crocodile?"

Billy G shook his head. "I don't even want to think about it. That would be a very horrible way to die, Ms. Jenny."

"Am telling you, Billy G, a would rather end up in a KFC family bucket, barbeque, or French fry."

"No, Jenny," said Jacko, standing up. "Your meat can't French fry, you too ole, them would have to boil your meat like dry peas, probly soak it from overnight."

All the animals and birds laughed at Jacko's potshot at Jenny. Jenny looked like she was going to swell and burst. All her feathers were fluffed up in the air. "You see what a saying, Billy G? Jacko, of all people, don't take this thing serious." She turned and faced all the animals and birds in the cave. "You know what a notice with some people when it come on to violence, it have to happen to them directly or them family before them take it serious."

Billy G took a step to the venting hen. "I understand what you are saying, Jenny, I'm going to address—"

"Let mi finish talk, Billy," said Jenny. "Violence have to hit close to home, or directly in a them home, before they feel how other people feel, them—"

"Okay, Jenny, take it easy," said Billy G, doing his best to calm her down. "We are going to come up with a solution to this animal cruelty problem we are all facing."

Jenny was huffing and puffing like an old steam engine. She looked across at Jacko and swore under her breath. She flew on one of the bamboo perches in the roof of the cave to cool off.

Gramps, the one-legged rooster who was a few inches away from Jenny on the same perch, hopped on his one leg and drew close beside her. "Don't pay Jacko any attention, baby, big papa is here to relief you stress," he said, putting a wing around her.

"Clear off!" said Jenny, pushing Gramps away from her. "Don't sorry for mi, with you one foot."

Gramps hopped back to his original position on the perch and turned to a few birds that were watching the fiasco. "Is a rooster she want in her life, that's why she is so miserable."

They all wanted to laugh, but they saw that Billy G was not in the mood for their antics.

Billy G turned to Jacko. "Jacko, Jenny has a point, this is not a laughing matter. So please ease off the jiving."

Billy G could feel the pressure mounting on his shoulders. He knew the animals and birds were depending on him and the committee to come up with a strategy to solve their problem. He felt that they should all work as a team. He looked at them all once more. "If anybody has a suggestion for how we can tackle this problem, the floor is open," he said.

All the animals and birds began to murmur among themselves. Billy G waited for a half minute before he spoke again. "Come on, gentle peeps, I just want to hear your suggestions before the committee says ours—"

"I and I man say we should burn out all wicked humans!" shouted a voice, coming from the entrance of the cave. "Put a fire on all humans who cruel to animals!"

Everyone turned their heads toward the entrance of the cave where they saw Ras Blah Blah, the only sheep on the island that had black wool. He had run away from a nearby sheep farm because he did not want the farmer to shear his wool. Huge clumps of unsheared wool clung to his body, giving him an unkempt look. He was the only animal in the community who believed in the Rastafarian religion. Some of the animals and birds believed that he was slightly sick in the head, while some of them believed that some of what he said made sense. He usually annoyed Hebrew, who was of the Christian faith, with his Rasta talk at times.

"Welcome to the meeting, Ras, just keep you voice down a little," said Billy G, wishing in his mind that Ras Blah Blah had not shown up for the meeting. The Rasta sheep was always an instant distraction in the meetings he had attended in the past.

"Nooo, Billy, is that Babylon want we to do, keep our voice down, but we voice going be heard!" shouted Ras Blah Blah.

"O Jesus, help us, Lord," said Hebrew under her breath.

Ras Blah Blah walked to the front of the crowd and stopped beside Billy G.

Billy G didn't have time for the Rasta sheep and his usual preaching. "I hear you, Ras, anyway, we trying to come up with a solution to defend ourselves from the humans."

"You don't hear what the I say we should do?" asked Ras Blah Blah. He faced the crowd and started to move about like a performer on a stage. "Put a fire on all human evil creation—fire on a slaughterhouse, fire on a dairy farm, fire on all pharmaceutical company who a use lab rat and guinea pig to test them deadicine. Fire!"

Billy G was surprised when some of the animals and birds started to support Ras Blah Blah's fiery idea. "Yes, Billy," said War Plane, from one of the perches overhead, "let Cutter, the rat, gnaw off the electric wiring in Lanky Roy and Yabba house and start a fire."

A few other birds in the crowd joined War Plane and started to support Ras Blah Blah's idea, the very thing that Billy G was trying to avoid.

Billy shook his head at the riling crowd. "Gentle peeps, the committee cannot sanction that kind of behavior."

"Why?" asked one of the teenage male goats at the back of the cave.

"Because there is a young human baby in Lanky Roy's house," said Billy G, "and the baby is innocent." He turned and pointed to the two kids that were resting beside their mother. "How would you feel if you heard that the humans set fire to those two kiddy goats over there?"

Hebrew nodded. "Yes, that is true. Jesus, say we must not render evil for evil."

Billy G felt relieved that he had at least one person on his side. "Furthermore, if we start a fire," he said, "it probably spreads to a neighbor's house, and not all humans are like Lanky Roy and Yabba. Some of them actually love us."

"Is what the I saying, Billy?" asked Ras Blah Blah, turning to the crowd. "Most of them humans a hypocrite. Them act like them love animals, especially some who call themselves Rasta."

"A true, Ras!" shouted Grunty, the pig.

"Rascal, I call them, Grunty," said Ras Blah Blah. "Some of them Rastafarian humans claim them don't wear notting that make out a animal skin. No belt, no jacket, no shoes . . . and at the same time, you see them a chant and a beat drums that make out of goatskin, fire!"

Billy G rose up on his two hind legs and stamped both of his front feet hard on the ground. "Okay, Ras, that's enough!"

"One more point the I have to make before the I finish talk, Billy G."

"Make you last point fast," said Billy G, "because time is going."

Ras Blah Blah looked up at the perch where Jenny, Gramps, and some of the other birds were sitting. "Look on the commercial layer fowls them," he said. "Them lay most a them life for them human masters, and once them laying bag go on redundant, what them get for them years a service?"

"A retirement package!" shouted No-Shame, the John Crow, who was sitting at one end of a perch by himself.

"Retirement package?" asked Ras Blah Blah. "Them get a one-way trip to the nearest slaughterhouse, a knife to the neck. Straight to the curry pot."

"True word, Ras," said Gramps. "Them humans need a good lesson."

Ras Blah Blah turned to Billy G. "I and I man done talk." He walked to the back of the crowd and sat among Jacko's group.

"Listen, gentle peeps," said Billy G, shaking his head. "You all seem to be in this blood for blood vibes, but the committee doesn't work like that." He turned to the rest of the committee board members. "Listen, gentle peeps, myself and the committee think we should warn Lanky Roy that if him—"

"What kinda warning you talking about, Billy?" asked the mother goat.

"The only way humans don't mess with a animal or bird, is if them know them will get kill or serious damage from that animal or bird."

"True word, sister," said Guana, the green lizard, who was relaxing on one of the cave's walls. "Because anytime I change my skin from green to black, them stay far from mi."

All the animals and birds started to laugh at Guana's self-praise comment, but Billy G quieted them with the raising of a front hoof.

"Glad you understand what am saying, Guana," said the mother goat. "A can bet you that if Mongrel was a pit bull, them humans wouldn't mess with him."

They all had no choice but to agree with the mother goat. They all started to whisper to one another. Billy G felt a little better how the meeting was coming on. He took a deep breath and exhaled softly. "Look here, gentle peeps," he said, "violence is not the solution to a problem—"

"We have to defend our self, Billy!" shouted a red-tailed hawk from one of the overhead perches.

Billy G planted his four hoofs on the ground and looked at the hawk that everyone in the community called Chicken Hawk. "Violence and self- defense are two different things, my friend," he said. He looked away from Chicken Hawk and looked at the entire group of animals, insects, and birds. "And is not only us on the island have these kinds of problems." He turned toward the pair of Kling Kling blackbirds in the visitor's section. "These two blackbirds are from the parish of Manchester. They had to leave their home because the human government approved bauxite mining on a piece of land close to their treehouse."

"That is very sad," said Hebrew.

"Yes, it is," said Billy G. "They had to leave because of the caustic dust caused by the bauxite mining." He pointed a hoof at the crowd. "And bear in mind that these birds are endangered species. They have been forced out of their home because of the same human government that is supposed to protect them."

Ras Blah Blah looked at the two Kling Kling blackbirds, "A so Babylon stay. Sorry to hear that, idrin and sistren." He turned his head toward the doctor bird. "What problem the I have?"

The doctor bird cleared his throat and looked shyly at the crowd. "Hello, my name is Doc," he said. "Am from Clarendon. I was living in a sweetsop tree with my entire family. Two weeks ago, a loud noise wake me up—"

"Was it a earthquake?" asked No-Shame.

"A wish it was," said Doc. "I looked down and see that it was a bulldozer.

A male human was driving it, and—"

"A bulldozer under you treehouse?" asked Jack Hammer, the woodpecker.

Doc nodded. "Yes, the human was bulldozing every tree in the area. So a lost my house. Two of my family members died that day, a cousin and a sister."

All the animals and birds were saddened by the doctor bird's loss. A few looked away while shaking their heads. Some of them looked as if they wanted to cry. A teardrop fell from Jenny's eyes. "That's so sad," she said.

"Yes," said Doc, wiping his eye with a wing. "The next day, a learn that they were getting ready to build a new highway."

"Can you imagine that?" asked a ground dove. "And the human government have the nerves to call you their national bird."

"That's just a title, my friend," said Doc. "It comes with no benefit, other than having my picture on their lousy currency and a few mailing stamps."

Ras Blah Blah stood up. "Government again, Babylon again. People, if them don't care for them own a humans who vote for them, how them going care for us?"

"Real talk, natty!" shouted Gramps, the one-legged rooster.

The support from the handicapped rooster boosted Ras Blah Blah even more. "Them classify some a us as endangered species, but them is a dangerous species, fire!"

One of the menacing mongrel dogs from the Hungry Belly Crew stood up. "A true, Ras," he said. "A who say you don't have any sense?"

Most of the animals and birds took side with the Rasta sheep. It was the first time most of them agreed what he was saying was true.

Billy G did not like the idea that Ras Blah Blah was getting all that support; he lifted his right front hoof in the air and called their attention to him. "Okay, gentle peeps, keep it down!" He turned to the rest of his committee board members and looked at the female mule. "Gentle peeps, Muliesha has a good suggestion. I want all of your opinions on it."

Muliesha rose from her sitting position and cleared her throat while looking at the crowd. "Well am, I suggest we that we all should—"

Out of nowhere, Mouth-a-Massi, the talkative parrot, flew into the cave. He pitched on the ground beside Billy G. The parrot was breathing hard, and the feathers on his face were ruffled; he looked like he had just seen a ghost. Billy G stepped to him with a perplexed look on his face. "What is the matter, Mouth? Did you leave to eat some of those godforsaken seeds that always make you high?"

"No, Billy, something is about to happen, and a can't believe . . . I—"

"You can't believe what?"

Billy G and the others didn't understand Mouth-a-Massi's strange behavior. The parrot was sitting on the ground, looking at Billy G wide-eyed.

Gramps shouted, "Ease off the weed seed, Mouth Almighty!"

Some of the birds began to laugh at the parrot.

Billy G gave Gramps a warning stare by staring at him over the rim of his old eyeglass frame. "Calm down, gentle peeps!" he said, turning to the parrot. "What you can't believe, Mouth, what did you see or hear?"

"Billy G," said Mouth-a-Massi, "I fly out to do a quick dropping because as you know, one of the rule is not to doo-doo in—"

"I'm aware of the rules, Mouth. I set them, remember? Now tell us all what got you so freaked out."

Mouth-a-Massi looked at the crowd and began to explain. "Um, people, a was just coming back from relieving mi self when a see Kas Kas—"

"You mean that pigeon who love to spread rumors?" asked Billy G.

Mouth-a-Massi nodded. "Yes, she said she see and hear Speng Shell give Lanky Roy instructions to get rid of all stray animals in the area. She say Speng Shell even start pay Lank Roy already, and him don't start the job yet."

All the birds and animals looked at Mouth-a-Massi as if he was stupid. Some of them even began to get upset with him.

"You really fall in a Kas Kas rumor trap, Mouth-a-Massi?" asked Chicken Hawk. "A don't expect better from you still."

Grunty shouted, "The Mongrel bite-off-foot thing never work, so she roast up another rumor!"

Billy G looked at the crowd of animals and birds and shook his head. "Gentle peeps, give me a moment." He turned back to Mouth-a-Massi. "Where is Kas Kas now?"

Mouth-a-Massi pointed his right wing toward the mouth of the cave. "She outside, she say she is afraid to come in because you not going believe her. She say she know she lie about Mongrel two back foot."

"She lied about a lot of other things," said Billy G. "Go and tell Stinger to let her in."

Mouth-a-Massi quickly flew outside to get Kas Kas.

Billy G turned to the crowd. "Gentle peeps, please don't say anything to Kas Kas," he said. "If I find that she is lying, then she deserves to be put in her place, but I will do that."

The sounds of beating wings were heard coming from the entrance of the cave. Everybody looked to the entrance where they saw Stinger, the leader of the wasps, flying slowly about three feet off the ground. Below his beating wings, they saw Kas Kas walking slowly to the front of the crowd. She was dragging her feet as if she had lost all her strength. The male Kling Kling blackbird jumped off his perch from the visitor's section and offered his seat to Kas Kas. She accepted the seat and looked down on the ground. She was too embarrassed to look at the others.

Billy G slowly walked up to Kas Kas and spoke to her gently. "Kas, the story that you told Mouth-a-Massi, is it true?"

Kas Kas nodded and looked at Mouth-a-Massi as he flew back in the cave and perched on the ground beside Billy G.

"Yes, Sir Billy," said Kas Kas, "the story that a tell Mouth-a-Massi is true."

"Lie she telling!" shouted Lorna, the pregnant mongrel dog. "Is same way she spread rumor that is six different bull dog a pregnant for."

"Oh please, Lorna," said one of the menacing mongrel dogs. "Everybody know that anytime you in heat, the entire bull dog population rush your body—"

"Watch you language!" shouted Billy G. He pointed to the two kids. "You realized that kids are here?"

There were small giggles throughout the crowd, but everybody tried to keep their giggling from turning into a laugh. No one wanted to upset Billy G at that moment. Billy G turned his attention back to Kas Kas. "You see, Kas, it is very hard for us to tell if you are speaking the truth—"

"A telling the truth, Billy G."

Billy G scratched his forehead with a hoof. "Yes, Kas, but after so much false story from you, not to mention the one today about the croc biting off Mongrel two back feet, how you expect us to believe you now?"

Kas Kas looked like she was close to tears. "Billy G, as God, mi not lying."

Billy G shook his head. "We hear the god-swearing phrase already, Kas, probably you going to have to take God off the cross before some of these peeps believe you tonight."

"Sir Billy, if am lying this time, I want you and everybody in here to—"

"I'm sorry, Kas Kas, you gave us no choice, a mean just put yourself in our position. Cool off and enjoy the rest of the meeting." He turned to Muliesha and motioned with a hoof for her to resume what she was going to suggest to the crowd before Mouth-a-Massi interrupted her.

Muliesha stood up and cleared her throat again. "As I was saying before, I think we all should —"

She was interrupted by a soft swooshing sound that entered the cave. She looked up to see a huge male owl that everybody in the community called Patoo flying toward her. Patoo landed beside Kas Kas on the visitor's perch.

Billy G frowned at the owl. "Patoo, why did you choose to interrupt the meeting and sit on the visitor's perch?"

Most of the birds endorsed Billy G's comment by nodding and looking at Patoo. They felt like he should have perched on the regular perch they were sitting on.

Patoo looked at the crowd and pointed a wing at the perch he was sitting on. "Is this bamboo perch you all a worry 'bout?" he asked.

"What is your point?" asked Billy G.

"My point Billy, G," said Patoo, "is that, you all worrying about a stupid bamboo perch while Lanky Roy and Yabba is out rounding up all sick and stray animals."

The entire cave was frozen in silence; if another tear had fallen from Jenny's eyes, everybody would have heard it.

Kas Kas looked at Billy G. "Them was supposed to start tomorrow," she said. "Speng Shell say is tomorrow night."

Billy G looked back and forth from Kas Kas to Patoo. "How did you get this information, Patoo?"

"A have a girlfriend who live in a bissy tree, close by Lanky Roy house," said Patoo. "So a went to look for her. A was flying pass and see Lanky and Yabba with a animal in a cage."

Billy G shook his head; it's as if his brain had refused to comprehend what the owl had told him. "You . . . you mean they actually have a captured animal in their possession?"

"You make that sound nice, Billy G," said Patoo. "Them not only have a animal in their possession, them have a sick cat in a metal trap."

The entire cave began to panic. The birds were shifting and shuffling on their perches. Nanny Stush, Hebrew, and most of the female animals were all looking scared. All eyes were on Billy G, but he was too stunned to speak. He looked toward his fellow board members, but they also were looking scared. Muliesha quickly sat down. She knew that her suggestion wasn't going to help in a situation like that. The huge Red Poll bull that was sitting beside her looked as if he was about to choke on his cud.

Without hesitation, Jacko got up and ran to the front of the cave. He turned to the crowd and pleaded for them to give him a moment to speak. "Calm down! Calm down!" he shouted.

They all began to quiet down. They knew that Jacko always had good suggestions, but they doubted he could help in that situation. It was the biggest dilemma the animal community had faced since the Cross Roads dog-soup crisis.

Jacko turned to the president of the Animal Committee. "Hear mi out for a moment, Billy. I have a idea for a plan, but for the plan to work, we need a rat, a woodpecker, and a owl."

Patoo raised his right wing in the air. "You have mi already, man."

"Thanks for volunteering," said Jacko, turning to the crowd. "Get mi Jack Hammer and cutter now."

Jack Hammer flew from the perch he was on and landed beside Jacko. They all turned around looking for Cutter, the rat, but he was nowhere to be found.

"Where is Cutter?" asked Billy G.

Jacko replied, "Him was out front earlier when Mongrel come."

Mouth-a-Massi flopped both of his wings to get everyone's attention. "Hey, when a go outside to take a latrine break earlier on, a see Cutter on top of a bunch a ripe banana—"

"On top a my bunch a ripe banana?" asked Jacko. "A don't want any rat mouth on mi food."

"Too late, him all most done it," said Mouth-a-Massi.

Billy G shook his head. "Mouth, please go and tell Cutter that I need him in here now."

Mouth-a-Massi nodded. "No prob, a will do that." He flew toward the entrance of the cave.

Gramps laughed at the talkative parrot. "Hurry up, informer!" he shouted.

Mouth-a-Massi ignored the name-calling from the old rooster and exited the cave.

Billy G paced the floor while he waited for Mouth-a-Massi to return with Cutter. As the president and leader of the Animal Committee, he felt as if he was losing his grip on his community.

A few minutes after, they all watched as Cutter strolled across the cave floor. His belly was swollen from the amount of ripe banana he had eaten. Billy looked at the oversized rat and shook his head. "Cutter, a can't believe you outside stuffing you belly while we inside trying to solve this problem facing us."

The overstuffed rat patted his belly and looked at the president of the Animal Committee. "Food come first, Billy. A hungry soldier can't go to war," he said, looking at Jacko out of the corner of his eye. "What you call mi for now?"

"Oh god, give me faith," said Billy G, shaking his head. "Jacko has something to say to us all."

Jacko wanted to give Cutter a piece of his mind, but he kept his cool. "Okay, this is the plan," he said, looking at Jack Hammer, Patoo, and Cutter. "This is what you three going do." They all drew closer to the spider and listened as he explained his plan to them.

CHAPTER TWELVE

Dusk had started to settle on the Johnson Lane Housing Scheme. Lanky Roy sat on the step of his veranda, eating a plate of curry chicken and white rice. He took a long drink from a glass of lemonade that he had in front of him. He rested the glass beside him on the veranda step and looked at Yabba, who was sitting close by on the crossbar of an old BMX bicycle.

Yabba was holding his right ear. The swelling of the ear had reduced, but it was still visibly larger than the other ear. A puny-looking brown cat was lying in a three-by-three square-shaped steel cage that was on the ground between both men. The cage had the resemblance of a homemade birdcage. A two-inch nail secured a small latch on the front of the cage. The helpless cat looked at its two captors while they laughed and talked. "A can't believe that the five a'clock news never show mi face," said Lanky Roy. "Mi vex, man."

"A true, mon," Yabba agreed. "Speng Shell say you would star the news tonight, but a mongrel face alone the news show."

Lanky Roy spat out a piece of chicken bone on to his plate. "What the TV station think, that a wouldn't want people to see mi face?"

"Them probly don't show you face because them know them animal rights people would take it make a big thing."

Lanky Roy scooped up a forkful of rice and looked at his friend. "Them act like is a human being a was dashing in the river. Can't believe people sorry for a mongrel dog."

"A true, mon," said Yabba, looking at the cat in the cage. "If them ever know you planning to make some real money off them stray animal in the area."

Lanky Roy froze with a fork full of rice halfway to his mouth. "How you mean *you*, why not *we*?" he asked. He emptied the rice that was on the fork back onto the plate and pointed the fork at Yabba. "Look, mi and you . . . *we* going make some money off them stray animals. Don't cop out on mi, Yab."

Yabba looked toward the gate to see if anybody was close by to hear his words and then leaned close to Lanky Roy. "No, mon, but mi 'fraid to get involve with Speng Shell. A mean, Speng Shell pop man hand and foot who don't carry out him orders, you know."

Lanky Roy looked at his friend and laughed. "A that scare you?"

"Of course. If is a wasp bite mi today and the pain so hot, can you imagine two pop hand and two pop foot?"

Lanky Roy took another drink from the glass of lemonade and then looked at his cowardly friend. "Is a easy job, Yabba," he said, twirling a few ice cubes that were in the glass. "Five grand per dog multiply by the amount a stray dog in the area. You know how much that, Yab?"

Yabba began to count on his fingers. "Um, ahh, let mi see. A hate math you know, mon. About twenty grand?"

"So, you saying is only four stray dog in the area?" asked Lanky Roy. "You figure is wrong, the amount is over fifty grand. And that is only dog price alone."

Yabba almost fell off the bicycle bar when he heard the estimated figure. The thought of sharing more than fifty thousand dollars between Lanky Roy and himself was more than enough to make him rethink Lanky Roy's offer. He rubbed his chin with his right hand while he thought it over. He got off the bicycle, laid it on the ground, and walked to Lanky Roy. "Am, who else know about Speng Shell offer?" he asked.

Lanky Roy spat a large piece of ice out of his mouth into his hand. "Only mi, you, and Peaches know about it."

"Good, that good. So what she say to you when you tell her about it?" asked Yabba.

Lanky Roy put down his plate on the step beside him. "You know how Peaches love money already."

"Yeah, a know." Yabba laughed. "All right, Lanky, a will come on board if you promise mi one thing."

"What?"

"Don't tell Speng Shell that mi help you. Tell him Clifton or somebody else help you, but don't mention mi involvement to that man. Deal?"

"Okay, boss, deal," said Lanky Roy. "Just make sure tomorrow when a ready to start capture the fowls, a don't get voice mail when a call you cell phone." Lanky Roy turned his head toward the front door that led to the inside of the house. "Clifton!" he shouted.

"Yes, Uncle," answered Clifton from inside the house.

"Put down the Bible and come here!" said Lanky Roy, turning to Yabba.

"From this evening, him start to read Bible, say him praying Mongrel find him way back home."

Clifton came out of the house and walked on the veranda. He had a small blue Bible hugged to his chest. He was looking sad and lonely. "Yes, Uncle."

"Scrape out them bone here and wash this plate now," said Lanky Roy. He took up his plate and handed it to the boy. "And fix you face. From that mongrel dog run away, is like half a your life gone. Get over it."

Clifton looked at the plate in his hand that had several pieces of chewed-up bone on it. He wrinkled his nose at the sight of the crushed bones and walked to the inside of the house.

Lanky Roy shook his head and turned to Yabba. "A wonder if a dead, that bwoy would grief over mi like how him grieving over the ole mongrel dog?"

"A doubt it." Yabba laughed. He walked back to the bicycle, picked it up off the ground, and sat on the crossbar.

"You just as bad," said Lanky Roy. "As a was saying, Peaches love the fact that money going make off this job. It was even her idea that a try out one of the cage tonight."

Yabba laughed in his mind. He knew that his friend's baby mother was a lover of money. He pointed at the cage in front of them. "Speng Shell, trick you and drop off the cage them from tonight."

"Test him testing mi, to see if a serious."

"But you take him money, so you must serious," said Yabba.

Lanky Roy felt his pocket and nodded. "Yeah, well a glad him drop the cage them off because a get to see that them work and that the puss fall for the chicken bone."

Yabba slapped at a mosquito on his hand. "The man tell you to use butter, and you use chicken bone."

"Speng Shell don't care about the bait," said Lanky Roy. "Him only care about the catch. Him wouldn't care if a cut off you big lip and use it as bait." Lanky Roy began to laugh at his friend.

"Go on laugh, mon, you realized you have a big problem?"

"What problem?" asked Lanky Roy.

"You agree to put the animal them in you car an' drive to meet the truck. You have battery in the car, mon?"

Lanky Roy put a hand to his mouth. "Rahtid, a was so glad about the job, a totally forget a need a battery." He looked at Yabba for a suggestion, but Yabba was looking worried.

"You can't give Speng Shell that excuse," said Yabba. "Him going say why you never tell him when you accept the job."

Realizing that he had an enormous problem on his shoulders, Lanky Roy got up off the veranda step and began to scratch the right side of his head. "Now what we going do, Yabba?"

"We?" asked Yabba. "You mean what you going do. The carbide thing not going work out for the mango."

Lanky Roy looked at Yabba. "Why?"

"A call a friend before a come over, him say the mango have to at least fit to carbide. Your mango them too young."

Lanky Roy scratched the right side of his head harder. "A bad lucky to rahtid. No money from mi sister, the mango them can't carbide, and the five grand can't buy a battery—"

"And you have a baby to feed," said Yabba, "rent to pay, and a baby mother who sound like she ready to leave you if you don't get some money soon."

"Thanks, Yabba, thanks to remind mi. What would I do without a friend like you?" said Lanky Roy sarcastically.

Both men stood in silence as they thought of a way to solve their predicament. After a few seconds, Yabba snapped his fingers. "Ahh, a have a idea, mon. You see the five grand that Speng Shell give you?"

"Yeah, what about it?" asked Lanky Roy.

"Give Pickah $500 out a it, and him will thief a battery for you. Him will glad, five bills will be like five grand to him."

A broad smile appeared across Lanky Roy's face. He welcomed Yabba's suggestion with open arms. "True word, Yab, good idea. We just need to find Pickah now. Him keeping low because Speng Shell say that him don't want any cokehead in the community, so—"

"Uncle," said a voice from the veranda.

Lanky Roy and Yabba turned toward the voice on the veranda. There they saw Clifton standing. He was shifting his weight from one foot to the next and fidgeting with the Bible in his hand.

"What the matter, Clifton?" asked Lanky Roy. "You do what a tell you to?"

"Yes, Uncle, but—"

"But what?"

Clifton started to fiddle with the end of his shirt. He didn't know how he was going to tell Lanky Roy what he had to tell him. "Um . . . the animals say you must let the sick cat go and that you mustn't carry out Speng Shell order."

"Animals?" asked Lanky Roy. He looked at Yabba, who was walking toward the veranda.

Yabba walked to the veranda and looked through one of the diamond-shaped spaces of the grille. "What you just say, Clifton?"

"A patoo just tell mi that the Animal Committee order you and Uncle to stop what you doing to the sick puss."

Lanky Roy could not believe the words Clifton was saying. "Patoo, Animal Committee? What you really saying to mi, bwoy?"

Clifton knew they were going to laugh at him, but he also knew that he had to play his part in order to help Mongrel and the rest of the animals. "Yes, Uncle," he said. "When a go round the back to wash out Putus food pan, a see the patoo. Him is around there right now."

"Around where?" asked Lanky Roy.

"At the house back, him said him waiting on a response from you."

Yabba held his belly and laughed until he almost cried. "Woi, him really mad, Lanky. You nephew head gone to rahtid."

"From the car knock him off the bicycle and him hit him head, him start talk to the mongrel dog," said Lanky Roy. "Now it look like him upgrade to bird." He walked past Clifton and stopped at the doorway. "Peaches, come here quick!" he shouted.

Peaches walked out of the house with her entire face covered with bleaching cream. She looked like a cross between a circus clown and something out of a B horror film. "What you hollering out mi name like that for, Lanky?" she asked.

"Clifton mad symptoms a get out a hand," said Lanky Roy. He told her what Clifton had told him and Yabba. When he was finished, Peaches looked at Clifton, walked up to him, and used the back of her right hand to feel the side of his neck and his forehead.

"What you doing?" asked Yabba.

"A testing to see if him have a fever. Mi granny always said if the fever get too strong and fly in you brain, it can cause you to talk foolishness."

Lanky Roy laughed and walked back to the step of the veranda and sat down. "The bwoy don't have no fever. A tell you him mad."

Clifton looked at the three adults. He didn't know what else to say in order to convince them that what he was saying was true. He walked off the veranda and stopped beside the steel cage. "Okay, Uncle," he said. "If you all don't believe mi, just follow mi around the back."

"Good idea, mon!" said Yabba mockingly. "Probly the patoo can show we where to find all the stray animal. Let's go, Lanky, we have a meeting with a patoo."

Peaches threw both her hands up in the air and rolled her eyes. "Okay, a will walk through the back door. You three walk around the side a the house," she said, walking into the house.

Lanky Roy told Clifton to lead the way. Clifton hesitated a little by looking at the puny cat in the cage. Lanky Roy used a hand and pushed him in his back and told him to move along. Clifton walked off while the two men followed him to the back of the house.

When they arrived at the back of the house, they saw Peaches with a warm-wet rag, wiping the bleaching cream off her face. She was also looking up at Patoo, who was perched on an upright iron bar that supported a clothesline. The clothesline was filled to capacity with wet clothes from the household. Peaches wiped a smear of cream off her forehead with the warm rag and stepped closer to Patoo. "A the first a seeing a owl so close up," she said, staring at Patoo's two huge hazel eyes. "It kinda look creepy though."

"Yeah, it ugly bad," said Lanky Roy, walking closer to the clothesline. It was a bit dark, but he could make out the dark brown feathers of the large bird.

Clifton walked up to Lanky Roy and pointed at Patoo. "See, a never lying, Uncle. The patoo is here, so you have to believe mi. Him not leaving till him get a answer."

Lanky Roy smiled at his nephew. "Okay, Clifton, him want a answer? I shall give him a answer." He began to feel the waist of his pants and then turned to Peaches. "Babe, look on top a the clothes basket you see the slingshot."

Peaches moved toward the back door of the kitchen, but Clifton quickly ran and blocked her way. "Noooo, Auntie, don't do it!" he yelled.

Peaches laughed and brushed Clifton aside with a hand. "Move out of mi way, bwoy."

There were sounds of flapping wings. The four humans looked up just as another owl and Jack Hammer, the woodpecker, flew into the backyard. Jack Hammer landed on the clothesline beside Patoo, but the other owl landed on top of a laundry room that was separated from the house. The owl was Patoo's girlfriend. Jacko had begged Patoo to ask her to guide Jack Hammer so he wouldn't get lost in the dark. There was a shuffling noise on top of the laundry room. Clifton looked toward the top of the laundry room and wondered why the owl had chosen to land there. He brushed the thought aside and walked to the upright bar of the clothesline where Patoo and Jack Hammer were perching. He looked up at Patoo. "What a must do, Patoo?" he asked.

The rest of humans looked at the male owl as its grayish- yellow beak move up and down. While its beak was moving, a soft hoo-hoo emitted from its mouth.

Lanky Roy looked at Yabba and shook his head. "What the—"

"Circus come to you backyard to rahtid, Lanky." Yabba laughed.

Peaches came through the kitchen back door and walked to Lanky Roy. "A don't see the slingshot, Lanky."

"Yeah?" said Lanky Roy. He scratched the right side of his head and walked to the kitchen door.

Before Lanky Roy reached the door of the kitchen, Clifton ended his conversation with Patoo and turned to him. "Um, Uncle, Patoo say if you don't believe mi, you must go and check the four tire on the car."

Lanky Roy stopped and looked at his baby mother and his friend. They were all looking confused by what Clifton had said. Lanky Roy looked at the large male owl and then looked at Clifton. "What mi car tires have to do with this, bwoy?"

"A don't know, Uncle," said Clifton, "but Patoo said like how you don't believe mi, you should check the tires."

Lanky Roy looked at Peaches and laughed. "You ever witness anything like this, babe?" he asked.

"Never in my life," said Peaches, turning to Yabba. "Yabba, go look and see if the fairy tooth lady thief the tires."

They all laughed as Yabba ran off to check the tires on the car. Peaches walked up to Clifton and pointed a finger in his face. "A carrying you to the doctor in the morning. You need medication, go finish wash out the dog pan and feed—"

"Blood fire! Lanky Roy, come look here!" shouted Yabba from the front of the gate. Peaches stopped talking to Clifton and looked at Lanky Roy, but the tall skinny man was already running toward the front of the yard.

Peaches looked at Clifton, but the only reaction she got from the little boy was a shrug. She walked past him to see what Yabba was creating so much excitement about.

*   *   *

Lanky Roy almost jumped over the gate. He quickly pushed it open and looked at Yabba, who was walking around the car and looking at the tires. The night was getting darker. From his position, Lanky Roy could barely see the right rear and front tires on the car. He walked up to the tires and looked at them. They were both flat like a pancake. Lanky Roy walked around to the other side of the car. A streetlight from across the street highlighted the damages to the other two tires on the car. They were also flat. Every ounce of air was out of each one. He noticed that there was a large drill-like hole on the outside of each tire. He stooped down and examined the hole on one of the tires with a finger.

Yabba looked at his lanky friend and shook his head. "Every tire have a hole in it, Lanky."

Lanky Roy stood up and clenched his fist. Like climbing vines on a concrete wall, every vein in his forehead stood up. He kicked at the ground with his shoe and cursed. "Any bwoy who puncture mi car tire going feel it. Them will have to answer to Speng Shell too!"

Peaches entered through the gate and walked to the station wagon. When she saw the flat tires on the car, her mouth was wide open. "No, man, something wrong, Lanky," she said, looking around to see if someone had punctured the tires and ran off. She turned around and saw Clifton standing at the gate with his Bible still in his hand. She shook her head and walked over to him. She held on to one of his arms and pulled him to the car while pointing to the flat tires. "Who puncture Lanky car tire? And don't give mi any patoo-do-it bull crap!"

"Is . . . is the woodpecker puncture them."

Peaches shook her head. "A don't believe mi ears. This a madness."

"Woodpecker?" said Lanky, walking to Clifton.

Clifton desperately tried to think of a way to prove that it was the woodpecker that had punctured the car tires and not a human. "Yes, Uncle," he said, "them have a committee that order the woodpecker and the owl to warn you and Yabba to stop what you doing."

Yabba looked at Clifton. He was a bit concerned. "And if we don't stop, what going happen?" he asked.

Clifton dug his right big toe into the dirt and picked at one end of the Bible with a fingernail. "Pa-Patoo say the puncture tire is only the beginning," he explained. "Him say if you and Uncle still plan to carry out the cruel act on the stray animals, worst things a go happen, and—"

"A don't believe this bull crap, Lanks," said Peaches. She looked at her baby father. "Let mi go look for the slingshot so you can show them birds our *beginning*." She walked to the gate, leaving Clifton looking helpless.

Yabba walked up to Lanky Roy and turned his back to Clifton. He didn't want to show the boy that he was a bit scared. "Lanky, suppose what the bwoy saying is true?" he whispered.

"Come on, Yabba, don't tell mi you believe a single word this idiot talking."

Yabba glanced at Clifton, scratched his chin, and looked back at Lanky. "Not really, but . . . you ever watch the *Dog Whisperer* on cable?"

"Yes," said Lanky Roy. "What the show have to do with this?"

"What if Clifton have the same gift that the man on the show have?"

Lanky Roy shook his head and walked away from Yabba and leaned on one side of the station wagon car. "A can't believe you fall for Clifton garbage, Yabba, trust mi."

"Uncle," said Clifton, walking up to him. "A true Yabba talking, a really can understand when a animal or bird talk, even cricket and spider."

There was a loud scream that sounded like it was coming from inside Lanky Roy's house. Lanky Roy ran off and opened the gate with such a force that it bounced back and forth on its rusty hinges. He ran into the house, calling out his baby mother's name. He found her at the back of the yard with her two hands covering her mouth. She was staring in shock at the clothes on the clothesline.

Clifton and Yabba had reached the back of the yard where they saw Peaches and Lanky Roy looking up at the clothesline. Sitting on top of the clothesline beside Jack Hammer and Patoo were Patoo's girlfriend and Cutter, the greedy rat. In his mouth, Cutter had a large piece of white fabric. Lanky Roy quickly ran inside and turned on the outside light. The light from the one-hundred-watt bulb showed the horror that took place on the clothesline during the short time they were gone. A very expensive- looking white long-sleeve Gucci shirt that was drying on the clothesline was filled with dozens of holes and ripped to threads. Lanky Roy looked at the large rat as bits of the shirt's fabric fell from its mouth. The rat was nibbling on what was left of the shirt's collar.

Lanky Roy could not believe his eyes. A rodent had destroyed the most expensive piece of clothing he had. The shirt had cost him a whopping seven thousand dollars, and he had only worn it once. Lanky Roy had planned to wear the shirt to an Independence Day party the following weekend and had told Peaches to rinse it out for him. He turned to her. "What happen, Peaches?" he asked.

Peaches could hardly speak. She didn't know where to start. "Um . . . um, when a come inside to look for the slingshot, a hear a ripping sound outside, so a come out to see what cause the sound, and this is what a see."

Lanky Roy began to look around on the ground as if he was looking for something. He spotted a stone the size of his fist nearby and picked it up. He lifted his arm and aimed the stone at Cutter, but Patoo quickly picked up the large rat with his feet and flew away. Patoo's girlfriend and Jack Hammer flew after him, and they all disappeared in the darkness of the night.

Lanky Roy lowered his arm, threw the stone on the ground, and walked up to Peaches. "Peaches, a can't believe you really hang out the shirt on the line with grease on it."

"Grease?" asked Peaches, looking at Lanky Roy as if that was the most ludicrous comment she has ever heard from him. "Lanky, for the five years a washing you clothes, you ever see a leave grease on any a them?"

"But that a the only time rat bite up clothes, when food grease on it, Peaches."

"Lanky, a wash you clothes with bleach, no grease never on the shirt when a hang it out this evening."

Lanky Roy walked away from her and sat on an old cement block that was at the side of the house. "What going on?" he said to himself.

Yabba walked to the clothesline. "You don't understand yet?" he asked. "You have a animal whisperer in you family. The puncture tire is one thing," he said, pulling the rat-bitten shirt off the line. "But this is something else."

Lanky Roy looked at Yabba. "So you saying the bwoy is right, and the animal them fighting back?"

"You want more evidence than this?" asked Yabba. He walked to Lanky Roy and dangled the damaged shirt in front of his face. "Look at the shirt. It look like a sieve to rahtid," he said, poking a finger through one of the holes in the shirt.

Lanky Roy got up and grabbed the shirt out of Yabba's hand. "Give mi the shirt and stop joke around. So what, you don't want the job no more?"

Yabba rubbed his chin while he thought of his answer. He didn't want to say no, but at the same time, he didn't want to say yes either. "Well, a want the money, mon, because the tire business slow." He pointed to the front of the yard. "Well, a mean, you have four puncture tire now." He laughed.

"Look here, this is no joke," said Lanky Roy. "Is either you in or out. If not, a will do the job alone.

Peaches walked to Lanky Roy and started to massage his shoulder. "Look, babe, probly you need to think this ting over—"

"Think what over?" said Lanky Roy, brushing away her hands off his shoulder. "You forget that you is the main reason why a take the job?"

"What you mean mi is the main reason why you take the job?

"How you mean what a mean?" asked Lanky Roy. "Because you can't satisfy, is a miracle a don't start break in a people house to support you."

Peaches inhaled a gulp of air and exhaled sharply. She felt like she wanted to smack him in the face. "Is my fault why you don't have a job? Is my fault why you sit down every month and wait on you sister to send money for her sick son, so you can use it to support you baby mother? Is my fault, Lanky Roy?"

Clifton, who was watching the episode all that time, quietly walked away and went inside the house through the kitchen back door. He didn't like to be around his uncle and Peaches when they were arguing.

Yabba turned his face away. He was a bit uncomfortable. He wished he hadn't come over that night. He didn't like it when Peaches and Lanky Roy vented at each other in front of him. "Yow, Lanky, a think a better leave," he said.

Lanky Roy looked at Yabba and held up a hand at him. "Hold on little, Yabba," he said, turning back to Peaches. "You very unfair, you know a need money for a battery in order to get the car back on the road—"

"Sell the ole car and buy a battery. You baby need tin feeding!" said Peaches. She stormed off and went into the house, slamming the kitchen door behind her with a loud bang that echoed throughout the housing scheme.

Lanky threw the shirt that he had in his hand on the ground and ran to the closed door. "Why you don't sell you bleaching cream and buy food for you pickney? Ugly like."

Yabba took a few steps back. He looked like he wanted to run out of the yard. "Blood fire, Lanky, you don't 'fraid she hear you?" he asked, looking at the closed door. "You better thank God she never hear you."

Lanky Roy walked to where he had thrown down the shirt and picked it up off the ground. "A don't care if she hear mi," he said.

"Well, mi care," said Yabba. "The next time you tell her hot words, do it when a not here . . . a don't want no blood splash on mi."

Lanky Roy walked to the clothesline and threw what was left of the shirt on the line. He walked away from the clothesline and walked past Yabba toward the front of the yard. "You in or you out, boss?" he asked without looking at Yabba. "You want make some money or what?"

"Yes, mon, a not jumping ship," said Yabba. "A mean, once a see the bird them fly away, after you was about to hit the rat with the stone, a realize that them is coward." He didn't want to admit to Lanky Roy that he was the one who was a coward.

"Okay, but a don't really buy into the animal-fighting-back ting," said Lanky Roy. They had both reached the front of the yard.

"A hear you, boss," said Yabba. He walked to the bicycle, picked it up off the ground, and sat on the seat.

Lanky Roy kneeled on one knee beside the steel cage that held the puny-looking cat. "A going give this puss some milk now because him worth a thousand dollars," he said, patting the cage with a palm of his hand.

"A true, mon, what we going do tomorrow again?"

"Only the fowls we can catch in the day with the rum-corn," said Lanky Roy, standing up. "We can't start capture the stray animals until in the night. A going store them in the washroom instead of the car. Don't really want people figure out what we doing."

"That make sense 'cause after this evening TV news, it better to keep it real low," said Yabba, gripping both handlebars of the bicycle.

Lanky looked at the cat in the cage. "Yes, because Mongrel done thief the spotlight."

"A don't care about fame, mon, a the money I want," said Yabba, pushing the bicycle forward. "Hide the cage with the puss, a will come link you about eleven a'clock in the morning so we can start round up the fowls."

Lanky Roy lifted up the cage with the cat. "Yeah, a going probly have to keep a eye on the animal whisperer all day tomorrow. So that him don't interfere with we plan."

"Good idea, mon," said Yabba. He rode off on the bicycle. When he reached the gate, he stopped and turned around to look at Lanky Roy. "Hey, Lanky," he said, "you can drop off the four tire at the shop when you ready, a will give you a nice discount." He laughed at his own joke and rode off, not knowing that the following day would be the worst day of his and Lanky Roy's lives.

CHAPTER THIRTEEN

Like tiny diamonds scattered on a black tablecloth, the stars glistened in the dark sky over the Ridge Mount Acres neighborhood. Member of Parliament Patrick Mullings sat on the lower veranda of the house, talking to his wife, Katrina. She was a very beautiful half-Indian, half-Negro woman who was in her early fifties. She had light brown skin and the looks of a former Miss Jamaica. Her shoulder-length hair was almost fully black, with just a few strands of gray hair on the top of her head. They were both sitting beside each other on a three-seat patio chair that was made entirely from wicker. A coffee table sat in front of them. The table was also made from wicker but had a rectangular-shaped glass for the top. Two white-and-gold imported chinaware cups and saucers sat on the table next to a matching coffee pot. The coffee pot was designed like an elephant sitting on its rump. Mullings took the elephant coffee pot by the handle and poured coffee into both cups on the table. Steam rose from the cups as the hot liquid flowed through the elephant's porcelain trunk into them. After he was finished pouring the coffee, the Member of Parliament handed his wife one of the cups. Katrina thanked her husband and smiled at him as she lifted the cup to her lips.

*   *   *

The sweet aroma from the steaming coffee drifted in the night breeze toward the noses of Thick Neck and Philip, the two bodyguards. They were both lingering close by on the lawn, talking while occasionally glancing toward the veranda. Thick Neck looked at Mullings sipping his coffee. The huge bodyguard wished he could have a cup of coffee, but his boss did not endorse social drinking with them and Katrina. He looked away as the MP started a conversation with his pretty wife.

*   *   *

103

"Hon, I'm so happy we got back Prinny," said Mullings, looking at a fluffy white female poodle that was curled up sleeping by Katrina's feet. "I don't know how Abigail would've coped."

About an hour before, an elderly man who lived in the neighborhood had returned the poodle to the Mullings' residence. Katrina, who had just gotten home from the hospital, was thankful to know that the dog was found and returned.

"The Lord works miracles, darling," said Katrina, resting her cup on the table. "He knows that our little grand princess would've worried herself to death if her pet was never found. We will have to let her know as soon as possible."

"You can do that in the morning when you bring her breakfast. She is going to be so happy. I have been cursing myself since yesterday afternoon for telling her the bad news."

"I don't know what you were thinking," said Katrina. "You could have worsened the child's asthma." She looked at the sleeping dog at her feet. "I wonder how Prinny got off the premises and ran that far."

"I think it was when those men were fixing the gate yesterday morning, she must have wandered through. We have to be more careful."

Katrina sighed. "Poor Mertle, she works so hard. We can't blame her for not seeing when Prinny left the house. Thanks to that kind gentleman. He deserved the reward."

The MP put an arm around his wife's shoulder and pulled her head to his chest. "That's true, but he refused the money. He said he was just being a Good Samaritan. Told me he kept Prinny until someone put out a missing picture of her."

"That's so nice of him. Don't have plenty of people like him in the world these days."

"That's true," said Mullings, stroking his wife's hair. "I can't believe that it was a stray mongrel dog that warded off that man from putting Prinny in his car."

Katrina lifted her head off her husband's chest and looked up at him. "A stray mongrel dog and what man?"

"The gentleman said he was driving yesterday morning when he saw a man trying to put Prinny in the back of a car."

"So, where was the mongrel dog, and what did it do to stop the culprit?" asked Katrina.

"The gentleman said the mongrel dog was walking beside Prinny and that it barked like crazy when the other man lifted up Prinny to put her in the car.

He said the culprit got scared and put down Prinny. Got in his car and sped off."

"Wow, that's amazing, darling," said Katrina, resting her head back on her husband's chest.

Mullings kissed the top of his wife's head. "That's true, honey. If it weren't for the mongrel dog, Prinny would've been out of our lives forever."

"May the good Lord bless that stray dog," said Katrina. "Speaking of mongrel, did you see the news this afternoon with those young men using that mongrel dog as bait to catch a crocodile?"

"Where did you watch the news?"

"I saw the news on the TV in one of the hospital's waiting rooms. It was disturbing."

"Yes, I caught part of that news," said Mullings. "It's so ironic that one mongrel dog saved Prinny and another was used as croc bait." He laughed.

"Why are you laughing, darling?" asked Katrina. "It's not funny. Those people in that community need to be educated about situations like those."

"I'm just taking a serious thing as a joke, honey. I didn't mean to laugh." He kissed her on the forehead.

Katrina looked up at her husband. "They need someone to talk to them. They will listen to you. You can make a difference."

Mullings nodded. "I agree," he said. He began to rub her shoulders tenderly. "I still can't believe that the stray dog defended Prinny." Mullings thought it was best to switch the focus of the conversation; he wasn't in the mood for one of his wife's lectures.

"Strange and unbelievable things happen in this world, darling. It's not impossible for a cat and a rat to be friends. It's called friendship."

"Yes, I remember when I was a boy, and I met the first white person. She—"

"Oh boy, here goes this story again." Katrina laughed.

"Come on," he said, playfully rubbing the top of her head with his chin. "It was a wonderful feeling. I felt different, important. You see, I never had a white person as a friend before. I would have done anything to protect her."

"Did you kiss her?" asked Katrina.

"Hon, I was five years old, and she was fifteen, remember?" Mullings laughed.

She turned her head to look at him. "I'm just teasing you, darling."

The Member of Parliament leaned over, kissed his wife on the lips, and gently eased her head off his chest. He poured himself another cup of coffee from the coffee pot. "Do you want more coffee, hon?" he asked.

Katrina shook her head. "No, darling, one cup is enough for tonight."

Mullings added a teaspoon of sugar to his coffee and stirred it while looking at Katrina. "Hon, can you believe that a business friend of mine called me tonight and told me that he wants to buy the part of the land that the cave is on?"

"Darling, can't we just have a good time, without you bringing up your work?"

"Hon," said Mullings, waving his free hand at the house and its spacious yard. "My work is what gives you all of this."

"I did not marry you for materialistic things, Patrick. I married you because I love you and if you don't know that after thirty years, then we have a big problem."

Mullings quickly put down his cup and hugged his wife. "I'm sorry, honey, I didn't mean it like that. Gosh, I know you're upset whenever you call me by my first name." He took his arms from around her and held both of her hands in his. "Honey, I am just anxious, that's all. I just want this project to come through so the pressure can ease off my head."

"What pressure?"

"The everyday pressure at work. Hon, look, after the construction and opening of these correctional homes, our party will look like a hero."

"A hero?" asked Katrina.

"Yes, I mean, look how many people are complaining that their juvenile family members have to be locked up or housed in the same facility along with other adult prisoners."

"And?"

"Hon, don't you see?" asked Mullings. "When the opposition was in power, they didn't think of building these homes for these troubled kids. All those people who are complaining will be happy, and I can guarantee they will vote for us next year."

Katrina looked down at her husband's hands that were holding hers and sighed deeply. "Patrick, there is more to life than personal gain. Why don't you think about those people in your constituency who need to be educated about animal cruelty?"

"Hon, are you going to annoy me every day with this mongrel-crocodile thing now? Please don't, I am begging you."

"So you're saying that I'm annoying, that I'm annoying you right now?" she asked, pulling her hands away from his. "What are they going to use next as croc bait, the mentally disturbed people on the streets?"

Mullings opened his mouth to say something and shook his head. He had a regretful look on his face. He was sorry that he had mentioned the *annoying* word. "Hon, I am sorry, I didn't—"

"Good night, Patrick," said Katrina, standing up. "I'm going to put up Prinny for the night and get ready for bed." She lifted the sleeping poodle off the floor and cradled it in her arms like a baby. She walked toward the main door that led to the inside of the house.

Mullings quickly got up and hurried after Katrina. He caught her by one of her shoulders and gently turned her around to face him. He looked at his two security personnel who were looking in his direction. "We're okay, guys, go take a smoke break. We will be going inside soon."

Thick Neck beckoned to Philip to follow him. They both stepped farther away from the veranda and lit a cigarette while they pretended to look at the stars.

Meanwhile, Mullings was on the veranda, pouring his heart out with apologies. "Honey, I'm so sorry if I upset you," he said. "You are right; money is not all. I agree that it's my duty to address issues like what took place on the riverside today. I promise that I will address it at the Independence Day speech next weekend, I promise."

Katrina was always hurt whenever she told her husband the truth. It always had a depressing effect on him, but she knew that it was for his own good. "I'm happy you see what I'm saying is true, and that I'm not annoying—"

"Oh no, honey, you are not annoying, never. I'm the stubborn one."

"Okay, darling," said Katrina. "I just want you to know that I care about you and also about the people who put us where we are."

"You're a hundred percent right, honey," said the MP. "I knew I made the right choice when I married you."

"Me too, darling," said Katrina, kissing him on his lips. "My mother always told me that no matter what you and your spouse have, never go to bed angry with each other. Let's get ready for bed." She held the dog with one arm and put her other arm around her husband's waist. She led him into the house as Thick Neck moved toward the coffee pot on the coffee table to finish what was left in it.

CHAPTER FOURTEEN

More peenie wallies had arrived in the cave, which made the inside much brighter than earlier on in the night. Patoo, Jack Hammer, and Cutter had returned to the cave. Patoo had just finished explaining to Billy G and the others what had taken place at Lanky Roy's house.

All the birds, animals, and insects were talking at the same time. The two birds and the rat had just confirmed their worst nightmare. To most of the older folks, it was more horrifying than the Cross Roads dog-soup crisis. Ras Blah Blah was calling for fire. War Plane was ready to attack Lanky Roy and Yabba even if it would cost him his life. Guana was ready to go on any mission that required him to prove his camouflage skill. Bruck Kitchen had decided that he was not leaving the cave, even if it was on fire. Both Hebrew and Nanny Stush were panicking, and the two Kling Kling blackbirds from Manchester had started to wonder if the caustic dust from the bauxite mining would be more tolerable than being captured and killed by humans. It was complete mayhem inside the cave.

Billy G held up a hoof toward the crowd and pleaded for silence. "Okay, gentle peeps, calm down, calm down," he said, walking through the crowd. He waited for them to quiet down before he continued to speak. "Gentle peeps, this is what we'll have to do." He looked around at all the fearful eyes staring at him. He let them wait in suspense for his suggestion. That was what Billy G loved the most. He enjoyed showing the animals, especially Ras Blah Blah, that he was the one who made the final decision even if it was Jacko or someone else that came up with the idea. After he felt that he had their undivided attention, he resumed his speech. "Because Clifton has spoken directly to Patoo in front of Lanky Roy, Yabba, and Peaches—"

"Not Peaches, Bleaches," said Gramps, the one-legged rooster. "Because is must Bleaches she name why she bleach out her face like that."

Jacko decided to join Gramps and his silliness. "And she always seem to forget the back of her ears and her two elbows," he said.

"Yes," said Gramps, "those part of her body black like midnight while her hands and face white like chalk."

There were snickers throughout the cave. Even Jenny, who was still perching overhead, looked like she wanted to smile. Billy G didn't like Gramps and Jacko's interruption. He was fuming. "Listen, gentle peeps!" he shouted. "This is no time to clown around. This is very serious, and we have to fight back, so let's plan this."

War Plane, the pechary bird, flew off his perch and landed beside Billy G. "I agree with you, Billy. A ready for the war . . . victory we going for," he said.

Billy G looked at the hot-tempered bird. "Yes, but in order to be victorious, we have to work together," he said, "which means, you will have to work in unity with No-Shame.

War Plane moved closer to Billy G; he didn't believe he heard the elderly goat right. "What you really say a have to work with that half-idiot John Crow?"

"Yes, that's what I said, War Plane," said the president of the Animal Committee. "You two will have to put your differences aside and work in harmony . . . brothers-in-arms."

"That going be very difficult, Billy G," said War Plane. He looked up at the perch where No-Shame was sitting. No-Shame lifted one of his wings and waved it mockingly at him. War Plane shook his head and flew back to his spot on the perch.

Billy G waited for War Plane to settle on the perch before he continued. "And that goes for everyone who has issues with their fellow animal or bird friends."

Everyone, including Lorna, the pregnant mongrel dog, looked at Kas Kas, who was still perching on the visitor's perch.

Kas Kas felt the sharp stares from the animals and birds. "A willing to work in harmony with everybody," she said, sinking low on the perch as if she expected a barrage of pebbles to be thrown at her.

"You don't get to decide that, Kas Kas," said Mongrel. He got up, walked up to the pigeon, and stood in front of the perch she was on. "But a forgive you and willing to work with you."

"Thanks, Mongrel," said Kas Kas, "a learn a good lesson today."

"What lesson is that?" asked Mongrel.

Kas Kas looked away from Mongrel and looked at the crowd. "The lesson a learn is . . . it not good to tell lie 'cause when you really telling the truth, people not going believe you."

Billy G walked to Mongrel and put a hoof around his neck. "That's very nice of you, Mongrel, you setting a good example here." He looked up at Kas Kas. "And thanks, Kas, not everyone has the guts to admit that they are wrong."

Kas Kas smiled and sat up fully on her perch. The praise from the wise old goat made her feel like she was part of the Animal Committee again. "Thanks, Billy," she said, turning to the others. "And a hope you all can forgive mi."

Lorna sighed and shook her head. "Healing take time, Kas Kas, but a will try," she said.

Jacko, Gramps, and a few others burst out in laughter. Billy G smiled and held up a hoof for them to calm down. "Okay, gentle peeps," he said after the laughing ended. "As I was saying, because Clifton spoke to Patoo in front of the humans, we can't use that as a surprise again. So we might have to continue working in collaboration with Clifton."

Jenny didn't like that suggestion; she flew off her perch and landed beside Billy G. "Billy, a not working with no humans. Furthermore, that bwoy Clifton make a remarks about mi one day that a never like."

Billy G looked up in the ceiling of the cave and shook his head as if he was asking God what to do at that moment. He couldn't believe what he was hearing. He looked at Jenny and sighed. "What remark Clifton make about you, Jenny?"

Jenny turned to the two Kling Kling blackbirds. She figured they would be more understanding because they were new in the area and that they were also birds. "One day, I lay a egg in Lanky Roy yard, and Clifton thief it—"

"That's not a remark," said Billy G, "that's a reaction caused by your action when you lay in the boy's yard." He shook his head. He didn't have time for Jenny's ridiculousness. "What was the remark, Jenny?"

"After him thief mi egg," said Jenny, "him say him rather eat common fowl egg than the one that sell in the supermarket. Out of order." She turned to the other birds on the perch overhead. "Is who him calling common fowl? Am a top-class chicken . . . pedigree."

"Pedi what?" Jacko laughed. "A hear of a pedigree dog, but I certainly never hear of a pedigree fowl."

That comment from Jacko got Jenny angry; she turned and stormed to the entrance of the cave. She was so angry that she had forgotten that it was night and that it was dark outside. She was near the entrance of the cave when Ras Blah Blah, the Rasta sheep, walked out in front of her and blocked her way. "Listen, lady, go back and sit down," he said. "We all in this ting together. Let a tell you something, sistren, you is a common fowl, accept who you are."

Jenny just stood there with her beak wide open, looking at Ras Blah Blah. He was the first one to talk to her in such a blunt manner. She felt overpowered; she was so shocked, she couldn't even move a feather.

Mongrel left from where he was and walked up to Jenny. "Jen, is true Ras talking. A mean, look at mi, people including you call mi Mongrel, and a answer because am a mongrel, and a accept it."

Ras Blah Blah stepped closer to Jenny. "Sistren, sorry, a never mean to be rude. The I just want you to know that Jah make you that way, and you should be proud of who you are."

Jenny was embarrassed that Ras Blah Blah was lecturing her in front of everyone. She slowly held her head to the ground and looked at her toes.

"Hold you head high, sister," said Ras Blah Blah. Jenny lifted her head and looked at the Rasta sheep.

"Don't try to be somebody else," Ras Blah Blah continued, "don't be like some of them humans, who don't like that they are black and bleach them skin to look white. Jah is against them for that."

Jenny nodded and smiled. "A get what you saying, Ras, we have no control over how we born."

"Good, I glad you overstand what the I is saying," said Ras Blah Blah. He walked to the front of the crowd and started to preach. "Now, idrens and sistrens, let us unite and work together to fight these humans."

Some of the birds flew to Ras Blah Blah and showed their support for the Rasta sheep by flying around him.

Most of the animals walked to the front of the cave and stood beside Ras Blah Blah. They began to pump their paws and hoofs in the air. They all wanted to go and attack the humans right away.

Bruck Kitchen didn't move from where he was at the back of the crowd.

Nanny Stush and Hebrew stayed where they were. Hebrew didn't like the fighting idea, so she stood up and addressed the crowd. "Excuse mi, brothers and sisters, let us forgive our enemies. The Lord said revenge is mine—"

"Yes, sistren," said Ras Blah Blah, "but remember, is Jah same one say an eye for an eye. And remember, Joshua and King David had to slay thousands a Jah enemies in order to protect the children of Israel."

"That's true," said Hebrew, "but a don't think—"

"Let mi ask you a question, sistren," said Ras Blah Blah, walking toward Hebrew. When he reached up to her, he stopped and looked her in her one good eye. "Is you two male humans run down a few nights ago, right?"

Hebrew looked around shyly at the crowd. She realized that she had to admit what had happened to her that night in Farmer Brown's banana field.

She didn't like the idea of discussing it with Ras Blah Blah, especially in front of all the birds and animals in the Iron Bridge community, but she couldn't lie about it. "Yes," she said, "it was mi them two male humans run down to kill mi for my meat—"

"How you know is kill them was going to kill you, sister?" asked Ras Blah Blah. He looked at the crowd and looked back at the female donkey. "How you know is not rape them was planning on raping you?"

Hebrew was utterly embarrassed by Ras Blah Blah's weird question. She couldn't even look at Nanny Stush. "What . . . what kind of question that, Ras?"

"A very good question, Hebrew," said Billy G, walking toward Hebrew and Ras Blah Blah. "It's not only one kind of cruelty we animals face from the humans. We sometimes face that kind of brutality from some sick male humans."

Lorna said, "The human authorities call it bestiality. That kinda thing happen from time to time, Hebrew."

"It happen all the time," said Ras Blah Blah, addressing the crowd. "The sick male humans have sex with cow, goat, donkey, even fowl." He turned to Jenny. "Sorry, Jenny, the I don't mean to get the sistren scared, but it happen regular on this island."

"Oh my god," said Nanny Stush. "I can't believe it."

"Believe it or not, lady," said Ras Blah Blah, "the last human them catch in one a them parish a have sex with a goat, him run leave him wallet and him house key. Him was so comfortable that him remove him personal belongings before him take advantage of the poor goat."

"Not to mention the donkey them rape in another parish a couple months ago," said Lorna. "A lady find her female donkey one morning with the donkey neck tie up to a breadfruit tree. Poor donkey couldn't even walk after her ordeal."

Hebrew stared at Lorna. She couldn't believe what the pregnant mongrel dog was saying. "You're not serious, Lorna?"

"As serious as a judge at a murder trial, Hebrew," said Lorna. "The perverted human even throw two ripe mango give the donkey. Bribe the poor donkey with ripe mango."

Jacko chuckled to himself and looked at Hebrew. "Careful, Hebrew, them will drop ripe mango for you."

Hebrew shook her head and sat down. "That a wickedness," she said.

Billy G nodded and pointed to Hebrew's right eye. "And don't forget your former human master hit you in one of your eyes and blind you." He walked back to the front of the crowd.

Ras Blah Blah followed behind Billy G and started his preaching again. "Animal cruelty comes in all form, idrens and sistrens. We have to do something about it!"

"Yes, we have to fight for justice, Ras!" shouted Chicken Hawk.

"A willing to die for mi freedom!" said War Plane.

The three menacing-looking mongrel dogs looked at each other and looked at the crowd. "The Hungry Belly Crew ready for the war!" they shouted simultaneously.

Doc, the doctor bird, flew off the visitor's perch and hovered in front of Billy G and the others. "A willing to volunteer, Ras," he said.

"The I help will be greatly appreciated," said Ras Blah Blah.

Doc turned to the two Kling Kling blackbirds, who were both looking uncertain. "What you two plan on doing?"

The male blackbird looked at his girlfriend, and she nodded her head at him. "Count us in, Doc," said the male blackbird, looking at Doc.

War Plane jumped in the air and started to fly around the cave and chant. "Fight to the death, fight to the death!" he chanted. Soon, most of the animals and birds started to chant with him. Even Mouth-a-Massi, who was coming back from one of his latrine breaks, was chanting too.

Meanwhile, Bruck Kitchen, the thieving cat, was at the back of the cave, observing the crowd. *Well, if you all think I going lose my nine life in this revolutionary war you all planning, you all making a big mistake,* he thought. He quietly stepped back a few inches.

Billy G looked around at the chanting crowd. He was happy that they had all decided to work together, but he was not so pleased that Ras Blah Blah played a major part in convincing the crowd to unite. He wasn't happy about that, but he had to keep his feelings to himself. He feared that if he externalized how he felt, the animals and birds would vote him out of his presidency position and give it to Ras Blah Blah. He couldn't allow that to happen, not while he was alive. He walked up to Ras Blah Blah and gave the sheep a hypocritical smile. "Thanks, Ras . . . for your input."

"No problem, man," said Ras Blah Blah. "Is Rasta duty to liberate the people, you know. I and I just doing Jah work."

Billy G nodded and swore in his mind that that was the last meeting Ras Blah Blah was going to attend. He turned to the crowd and cleared his throat. "Um, gentle peeps, let's plan how we are going to attack these humans." He began to suggest his idea to the crowd while Bruck Kitchen quietly slipped toward the entrance of the cave.

CHAPTER FIFTEEN

The hot sunlight pierced the glass of Lanky Roy's bedroom window and shone through an opening in the window's curtain. The skinny young man was lying on his side, fast asleep on a queen-sized bed. The crowing of a neighbor's rooster caused him to turn on his back. The sunlight from the window hit him directly in the face. Another crow from the rooster woke him up. He opened his eyes, and the heat from the sunlight burned his eyes. He turned his face away and looked at Peaches's side of the bed. There was only an impression in the mattress that her feet had left beside his head. He hated whenever they had an argument or a fight because she always went to bed with her face at the other end of the bed. The good thing about it was, most of the time, she would be less upset in the morning than the night before. He hoped that morning was one of those times.

He got up and walked over to Baby Tiffany's crib that was at the foot of the bed. He removed a large white mesh cloth that was draped over the crib and was used to protect his baby daughter from mosquitoes. The baby girl was fast asleep with her right big finger in her mouth. Seeing that Tiffany was okay, Lanky Roy put back the mesh over the crib. He walked to a clothesbasket in one corner of the room and took a pair of jeans that were resting on top of it. It was the same pair of jeans that he had on the day before. He put on the pants and removed a dark blue T-shirt from a dresser drawer.

After putting on the T-shirt, Lanky Roy walked through a small living room into a kitchen. The interior of the kitchen looked ordinary. A small wooden dining table, with four chairs around it, sat in the middle of the kitchen. The dining table was covered with a light yellow tablecloth. In one corner of the kitchen, there was a white single-door fridge. A long cupboard hung on a wall above the kitchen counter. Both the top of the kitchen counter and the cupboard were made from cheap medium-density fiberboard. Painted in a dull gray, they looked like they needed to be replaced. A tall plastic garbage bin with its top off stood on the floor beside the kitchen counter. The floor of the kitchen was covered with gray-and-white old- fashioned stone tiles. Peaches was in the kitchen, standing in front of a four- burner gas stove, preparing a meal. There were two pots on the stove: a saucepan with cooking oil in it and a large Jamaican Dutch pot filled with cooked dumplings and boiled green bananas.

Lanky Roy walked up to Peaches and gently hugged her from behind. Peaches eased him off by pushing him slightly with her right shoulder. "Almost twelve a'clock, and you just a get up out a bed. What a life you living, eh?"

Lanky Roy looked at a huge circular clock that was held to the fridge door by a magnet. "Twelve a'clock, so why you never wake mi up?" he asked. He had no idea he had overslept that late. Peaches walked away from the stove and started to cut onion, sweet pepper, and scallion on a cutting board that was on the kitchen counter.

"Lanky, I only wake up a man who have a steady job," she said. "You know, the kind of man who have a steady nine to five."

"Peaches, don't start the argument again. Money going make from this job. A can guarantee that."

"Seeing is believing, Lanky," said Peaches, adding the chopped ingredients from the cutting board to the hot saucepan on the stove. "When you have the money, a will convince."

"Ah, bwoy," said Lanky Roy. "Where is Clifton?"

Peaches added two seeds of pimento and a branch of thyme to the ingredients in the saucepan. "A send him a shop to buy a tin a Enfamil for Tiffy. If you never notice, her feeding finish."

"It done already?"

Peaches looked at him. "Yes, and a not in any mood to squeeze out any breast milk in her nipple bottle this morning."

"Then, babe, all you have to do is breastfeed her—"

"Hell no," said Peaches turning down the fire underneath the saucepan. "How much time a must tell you, a don't want mi two breast to reach mi knees before time?"

"But, babe, doctor said breastfeeding is the best—"

"The milk is the important thing, Lanky. That mean the baby don't have to suck the mother breast. That's why I squeeze it out in a bottle. You need to find a job where you baby can have tin feeding in abundance."

Lanky rubbed his forehead. He wished he could tell her about the five thousand dollars Speng Shell had given him the night before, but he wanted to save and buy a battery for the car.

"Things going work out, Peaches, trust mi," he said.

"Don't tell mi that, Lanky. Tell it to you daughter when she start cry for hunger when her feeding done."

Lanky Roy couldn't stand the argument any longer; the car needed more than a battery—it also needed four tires.

He dipped in his pants pocket and removed the five one-thousand bills and showed it to her. "Okay, babe," he said, "Speng Shell give mi this last night as a promise to him word."

Peaches looked at him and smiled. "You holding out on mi, Lanky?" She took the money out of his hands, rolled it together, and shoved it between her bosoms. "That's not a nice ting to do, Lanks. When a man hold out on a woman, the woman can do the same."

"Damn, a forget your motto, babe. No money, no love. May God help Tiffy."

"Leave mi daughter alone," she said, playfully smacking at him with a spatula that she had in her hand. He jumped out of the way and walked to the doorway that led from the kitchen to the living room. He stopped at the door's threshold and turned to her. The sweet aroma from the saucepan was making him hungry.

"Call mi when the food ready. A going brush mi teeth."

"Okay, man of the yard." Peaches laughed.

He chuckled to himself. "Peaches, a can't believe you send that bwoy to the shop, and you know we need to keep a eye on him all day."

"What you think him going do, run to call him animal friends to do more damage?" asked Peaches. She added a small bowl of cooked codfish flesh to the ingredient in the saucepan.

"No, a don't buy into that animal-communication foolishness," said Lanky Roy, looking in the direction of the clothesline. "A believe some form a grease accidentally spill on the shirt why the rat eat it up."

Peaches stirred the contents of the saucepan and turned up the fire under it. "But how you explain the car tires? Is grease accidentally spill on them too?"

Lanky Roy laughed. "Is that cokehead bwoy Pickah puncture the tires."

"Why would him do that?" asked Peaches.

"Because a threaten to shoot him with the slingshot yesterday evening. Him want to thief the mangoes off the tree."

Peaches looked at her baby's father and pointed the spatula in her hand at him. "You and Yabba need to teach him a lesson," she said, turning back to the saucepan on the stove. "Or tell Speng Shell so Speng Shell bwoys can give him a fine trashing."

"Yeah, but first, a need to pay him to thief a battery. Remember, the car need a battery to do the job, babe."

Peaches stopped what she was doing and looked at him. "Pay him with what?"

Lanky Roy didn't know how she was going to react, but he felt he had no choice but to tell her the truth. "A need back five hundred dollars out of the money to pay him."

"You lucky this five grand is already spend," said Peaches, adding a bowl of boiled ackee to the saucepan.

"Give the cokehead bwoy two dozen ackee off the tree to sell. Don't give him no money."

"Good idea, but a think him will prefer half dozen of the mango instead. Him beg mi two yesterday evening."

"The mango them green," said Peaches, "but a sure Pickah will find a way to ripe them."

Lanky Roy nodded. "Him probly carbide them."

"Probly," said Peaches. "What time Yabba coming over?"

"Good question, him was supposed to come from eleven a'clock. Leave breakfast for him." He walked off into the living room without waiting for a reply from her.

"Okay," said Peaches, "just don't tell mi to feed that puss you have in the washroom."

Lanky Roy stopped in his tracks. He had forgotten about the puny cat in the cage. He had left the cage in the laundry room among five other empty cages. He walked to the back door of the kitchen and pushed his feet in a pair of old flip-flops that were lying outside.

"Where you going?" asked Peaches.

"Nowhere, a just remember something," said Lanky Roy.

He walked to the laundry room, where he saw that the door of the laundry room was ajar. He pushed the door fully open and looked inside. All the other cages were on the floor of the laundry room the same way he had left them the previous night. The cage that the cat was left in was overturned on one of its sides, and the cat was not in it. The door of the cage was wide open. The two-inch nail that held the latch of the cage shut was lying on the floor a few feet from the cage.

Lanky Roy scratched the right side of his head. He couldn't believe the cat had escaped from the cage. He began to look around inside the laundry room. He looked behind and inside of a washing machine that was in one corner of the room. He looked under a small cupboard where Peaches kept the washing supplies, but all he saw were bottles of bleach, fabric softener, and various laundry detergents. He would have even looked into the clothes dryer if they had one, but the clothesline outside was the only dryer they had. The only thing that was in the laundry room other than the metal cages and washing machine was a long piece of rope that was behind the door. Lanky Roy ran out of the laundry room and ran into the kitchen where he saw Peaches sprinkling black pepper from a small plastic bag to the ackee and codfish. "Babe, you open the cage this morning?" he asked.

"Open cage?" asked Peaches. "A not even go in the washroom since morning. A only hear the puss a make noise this morning—"

"What kinda noise?" asked Lanky Roy.

"The regular sound a puss make when you lock it up too long."

Lanky Roy ran out of the kitchen and ran into the living room with the pair of flip-flop slippers still on his feet. In less than a minute, he ran back into the kitchen, talking on his cell phone. "Yow, Yabba," he said, walking out of the kitchen into the back of the yard. He began to look around for the cat. "Where you is, man? You was supposed to reach here from eleven. The puss gone." He took the phone from his ear and put Yabba on speakerphone while he continued to search for the missing cat. He walked to the root of the ackee tree and looked up in the tree to see if the cat was hiding in it. All he saw in the tree was its bright red fruits smiling down at him with their shiny black seeds and soft yellow flesh hanging from their branches.

"The puss is a actor, mon," said Yabba on the speakerphone. "It act like it sick in front a you, and as you turn you back, it MacGyver it way out a the cage. It outsmart you, Lanky."

"Yow, cut out the foolishness man," said Lanky Roy, "and just make haste and come so we can start the job." He hung up the phone without saying goodbye, just as Clifton limped into the kitchen with a tin of baby formula wrapped in a plastic bag. Lanky Roy followed his nephew inside the kitchen. Clifton rested the plastic bag with the baby formula on top of the kitchen counter. "See the feeding here." Without saying thank you, Peaches looked at the plastic bag with the tin of formula and looked at Clifton. "Just to run a the shop and buy one item, you take nearly a hour, mad-head pickney?" she asked.

Clifton hated whenever she called him a mad-head child. He felt like using a few expletives, but he swallowed his anger. "The shop was full a people, so a have to wait to get serve." He didn't want to stay and explain any further, so he walked away.

As Clifton walked past Lanky Roy and headed for the kitchen back door, Lanky Roy grabbed the boy's right shoulder and spun him around. Clifton tried to pull away from his uncle, but Lanky Roy held on to the collar of his shirt.

"Yow, bwoy, what you do with the puss?" he asked.

Clifton was tired of the physical and verbal abuse from both Lanky Roy and Peaches. He had had enough of it.

"Why you don't go look up under Peaches skirt, and you will see the puss," he said. He clenched his jaws, covered his face with his two hands while he waited for his abusive uncle to lash out at him.

"What!" said Peaches. She almost dropped the cover of the saucepan that she had in her hand. She could not believe that the little handicapped boy would make such a feisty comment. She advanced to him with her right palm raised to hit him, but Lanky Roy stopped her by grabbing on to her hand.

"Easy, babe, a will deal with him," said Lanky Roy. He pulled Clifton inside the living room by the front of his shirt and opened the door of a smaller bedroom. He pushed the boy inside the room. Clifton stumbled and fell backward on top of a single bed that was in one corner of the room.

Lanky Roy pointed at Clifton. "You going stay in there all day and night," he said. "No food for you feistiness!"

He pulled the door shut and locked it with a key that was in the outside door lock. He removed the key and put it in one of his front pants pockets. He heard a male voice outside and walked in the kitchen where he saw Yabba talking to Peaches. Yabba was sitting around the dining table. He was dressed in a pair of blue jeans and an old gray polo shirt. In one of his hands, he had a box of marbles, and in the other, he had a homemade slingshot. "This is for them birds, if them attack we," he said, waving the slingshot in the air. "Carry your slingshot too, mon."

Lanky Roy shook his head and laughed. "You really believe Clifton and this bird-attack thing, eh?"

"In some sort a way," Yabba answered, "a not taking no chances, mon."

"A hear you," said Lanky Roy. He wanted to tell Yabba that he thought he was just as crazy as Clifton, but he didn't want his friend to get upset and leave. He felt the job Speng Shell gave him required at least two people. He decided the best thing to do was to let Yabba think that he believed in Clifton's fairy tale. "Okay, Mr. Yabba in Wonderland," he said. "If them birds flee from a stone last night, them supposed to drop dead when them see two slingshots aiming at them."

"A true, mon, "said Yabba, looking at a plate of food that Peaches was dishing out. "Peaches, a can't believe the bwoy Clifton say that about you."

"Can you believe it, Yabba?" asked Peaches. "The bwoy very out of order, man."

"Him is more than out a order," said Yabba.

Lanky Roy removed a plate from a dish drainer that was on the kitchen counter and walked to the stove. "Is mi have to stop Peaches from knock him out."

"She should knock him out with a pot cover," said Yabba. "Feisty. Where him is?"

Lanky Roy cocked a big finger toward the living room. "A lock up the bwoy in him room. Him won't disturb we for the rest of the day."

"Serve him right," said Peaches. "Is just the mercy of God a going give him some food." She showed Yabba the plate of food that she had finished dishing out. "This is yours, Yabs, but it hot."

Yabba eyed the plate of food and licked his lips. "Thanks, let it cool out a little bit."

"Okay, no prob," said Peaches. She rested the plate of food on the kitchen counter. "It right here when you ready."

"Yeah, mon, thanks," said Yabba, looking at Lanky Roy.

He pointed in the direction of the laundry room. "What a way the puss escape out a Alcatraz, eh, Lanky?" He laughed. "Serious though, a thousand dollars that escape you know, mon."

"We will worry about the puss tonight, Yabba," said Lanky Roy. "A the fowl them we must focus on today." He put down a half-filled plate of food that he had in his hand on top of the kitchen counter and walked to the fridge. He removed a short, round Ovaltine glass jar from the top of the fridge and waved it in the air. The label was stripped from the jar, and it was filled with a clear liquid. There were about three dozen corn grains settled at the bottom of the jar. He walked to the dining table and handed Yabba the jar.

Yabba shook the jar in his hand and watched the corn grains danced up and down in the liquid. "A corn and what this, mon?"

Lanky Roy smiled. "That is corn grain, soak in the good ole white over-proof rum for the fowl them. It soaking from last night."

Yabba unscrewed the cover of the jar and sniffed the harsh scent of the rum. He quickly pulled his nose away as the strong alcoholic odor burned his nostrils. "Lanky, a you a the real big man," he said. "A can't wait to feed them hungry fowl and drunk them."

"And the pigeons them too." Lanky Roy laughed. He took the jar from Yabba, screwed the cover back on, and returned it to the top of the fridge. He turned to Yabba. "Them stray fowls will glad for the corn grains because them always hungry."

Yabba laughed and looked at the plate of food that Peaches had rested on the kitchen counter for him. "Yes, them always hungry, but right now, I hungry too." He got up from around the dining table and walked toward the plate of food on the kitchen counter.

Without warning, a large swarm of paper wasps flew into the kitchen from outside and surrounded the humans. Peaches let out a scream and dropped the heavy cover of the saucepan that she had in her hand. The heavy pot cover fell onto the hard kitchen floor and made a loud noise that echoed throughout the house. The noise was so loud that it woke up Baby Tiffany. The baby girl started to make a crying sound in her crib.

Dozens of wasps had poured into the kitchen. They covered the walls, the fridge, and the kitchen counter. Even some parts of the stove were covered with a blanket of wasps. With his two hands protecting his face and head, Yabba ran to the kitchen back door and tried to close it, but one of the wasps landed on his upper lip and stung him. The tire repairman bellowed in pain and held on to his mouth. He looked around and saw that there was no way out of the wasp trap he was caught in. He ran back to the dining table and hid beneath it. He quickly pulled the tablecloth off the table. The slingshot and box of marbles that he had rested on the table fell off and hit the floor. The box of marbles burst open, and some of the marbles fell out and rolled all over the kitchen floor. Yabba ignored the scattered marbles and hastily wrapped the tablecloth around his entire body. He left a small gap around his eyes so he could see what was going on. He looked like a frightened mummy.

Lanky Roy was lying flat on his belly on the warm floor. He looked at Peaches, who was close to him. She was sitting on the floor with her head tucked between her knees. He tried to reach a hand out to her, but a large wasp dove from the kitchen ceiling and flew toward his hand. Lanky Roy swiftly pulled his hand away from Peaches and hid both of his hands beneath his body. A few minutes after invading the kitchen, the wasps had finally settled down. The entire inside of the kitchen looked like a giant wasp hive. The wasps relaxed their beating wings and began to watch the three terrified humans.

*   *   *

Outside the door of the kitchen, Stinger and about two dozen of his security wasps flew around just in case one of the humans escaped from inside and tried to make a run for it. They all dodged out of the way as War Plane, the pechary bird, and Chicken Hawk flew out of nowhere and went inside the kitchen. Stinger's thugs looked at him.

"Yow, don't ask mi what that was all about," said Stinger, "must part a the ole Billy goat plan."

They all laughed and landed on the wall of the house to rest their wings while still keeping an eye on the doorway.

*   *   *

Inside the kitchen, several wasps that were on top of the kitchen counter cleared a section for the two birds. After War Plane landed on the counter, he looked at the humans and noticed that Clifton was not among them. Knowing that the humans in front of him didn't possess the gift of communicating with animals and birds, War Plane decided to use a strategy. He flew outside and returned shortly with one of Clifton's shirt in his beak. He had taken the shirt off the clothesline. He dropped the shirt on the ground in front of Lanky Roy and waited to see what the lanky human would do.

Realizing what the pechary bird's action signified, Lanky Roy looked at Yabba, who was peeping through the small gap in the tablecloth. Yabba nodded at Lanky Roy, hoping that his friend would do whatever the pechary wanted him to do. Lanky Roy got up and removed the key from his front pants pocket and walked to the living room. Yabba breathed a sigh of relief and gently touched his upper lip, which was getting fatter by the minute.

*   *   *

Inside the living room, Lanky Roy opened Clifton's bedroom door and looked at his nephew. Inside his bedroom, Clifton had a screwdriver in his hand. The ten-year-old boy looked like he was about to jimmy the door lock or take off the entire doorknob with the screwdriver.

"You bird friend them want you," said Lanky Roy, "them in the kitchen." He couldn't believe he had just said those words. He was happy Yabba was not in the room to hear him.

Clifton smiled and dropped the screwdriver on the floor. He walked out of the room with the smile still on his face. Lanky Roy's eyes grew red with anger as he watched Clifton walk past him. He wanted to squeeze the life out of the boy, but he was scared that if he put a hand on the child, the angry wasps in the kitchen would retaliate. The attack on Yabba's lip was a stern example of what they were capable of.

*   *   *

Inside the kitchen, Clifton ran to War Plane and began to talk to the bird. "What happen to Mongrel?" he asked.

War Plane replied, "Don't worry, Mongrel safe. Him is with the Animal Committee."

Clifton smiled at the owl. He felt like jumping for joy. After having a sleepless night, he was looking forward to reuniting with his best friend.

Lanky Roy watched Clifton from the living room doorway. He couldn't believe what was happening in his kitchen. His nephew was talking to a bird again, and the bird seemed to understand every word the boy was saying. Lanky Roy started to wonder if Yabba was smarter than he was.

After about a minute of human-to-bird conversation, Clifton turned around and faced Peaches, who was still sitting on the floor of the kitchen. "The pechary say him want you to go lie down in you bed," he said. He didn't wait for a reply from her. He walked to the kitchen counter and took the plate of food that Peaches had dished out for Yabba. "Him also say a should have a big plate a food."

Peaches looked at Lanky Roy and then looked at Clifton. "Lay down in which bed? You hear that a sleeping with bird?"

Chicken Hawk found Peaches' comment very offensive. He felt like he wanted to pull the false hair she was wearing off her head and throw it in the kitchen garbage bin. He was about to fly over to her, but War Plane held up a wing and stopped him.

War Plane didn't like Peaches' stubbornness, so he flew off the kitchen counter and landed on Clifton's right shoulder and began to talk into the boy's ear.

Clifton chewed on a piece of dumpling while he listened to the bird. After the bird had finished talking to him, Clifton turned to Peaches with a smile on his face. "Well," he said, walking toward her with War Plane still on his shoulder. "The pechary say if you don't go in the bed, him is going to instruct every John Crow in the community to pitch on the housetop—"

"What?" said Peaches. She looked at her baby's father, hoping he would tell her what to do.

Lanky Roy didn't know what to say to her. He just wanted to get out of the wasp-infested kitchen as soon as possible. Even though he wanted to leave the kitchen, he couldn't imagine having a single John Crow perching on his housetop. That would be very embarrassing for him and his baby mother. The entire housing scheme would probably think they were into obeah.

"Yes," said Clifton, "him say, you know that it is a disgrace in Jamaica if one John Crow land on a person housetop, much less six dozen." He walked to the stove. The wasps that were on the stove shifted to one side and allowed him to uncover the saucepan. He dished more of the ackee and codfish onto his plate.

Yabba shifted the tablecloth from his eyes and peeped out from under the table. His upper lip had tripled its original size. "Do what the bird say, Peaches," he pleaded.

Seeing that Peaches had decided to play tough, War Plane flew off Clifton's shoulder and exited the kitchen. In about ten seconds, he returned with No-Shame, the John Crow.

No-Shame flew into the kitchen behind War Plane and landed on top of the Dutch pot on the stove. The cover of the large pot shifted under his weight, causing him to lose his balance. No-Shame's loss of balance caused him to fall. As he fell, he accidentally knocked over the entire pot of food. Boiled green bananas, dumplings, and hot water spilled all over the stove and floor. One of the dumplings fell onto the floor and rolled toward Peaches like a cart-wheel. It came to a stop between her legs.

"Oops," said No-Shame, "that dumpling is a naughty little dumpling."

War Plane looked at No-Shame and shook his head. He knew when he had agreed to work with the John Crow, he was making a big mistake, but he had no choice. Billy G was adamant that they should work together; the old goat was making an example out of them both. War Plane hated that, but he tried to put his feelings aside and focused on the task at hand. He turned and mouthed a few words to Clifton.

Clifton walked to Peaches and pointed at No-Shame. "The pechary say, this a just one out of many John Crow. Five dozen and eleven is on standby."

Peaches did not want such disgrace to befall upon her and her baby. Six dozen black-feathered vultures on top of the house would draw the attention of the entire island. She slowly got up and walked to her and Lanky Roy's bedroom. A large swarm of the paper wasps flew in behind her.

Not taking any chances with Lanky Roy and Yabba, Clifton pulled up the kitchen back door and locked it with a key that was in the lock. He removed the key from the lock and put it in one of his pants pockets. He walked inside his uncle's bedroom, where he saw Peaches lying in the middle of the bed. The huge swarm of wasps that had followed her inside had surrounded her. They were on the sides and edges of the bed. They were also on the window that was above the bed's headboard. They were making sure she did not move to cause any problem with the Animal Committee's plan.

Baby Tiffany started to cry in her crib again. War Plane, who was perched on top of the dresser in the room, turned to Clifton. "Take up the baby and give her to her mother so she can breastfeed her," he said. He looked at all the wasps in the room and flapped his wings three times to get their attention.

"Hey, none of you should land on or touch the human baby," he said, "that's an order from Billy G and Stinger."

"Good," said Clifton, "a respect that advice."

"Me too," said War Plane, turning to Clifton. "Cliff, leave a few of them soft cotton looking am . . . am—"

"Diaper," said Clifton, lifting out Baby Tiffy out of her crib.

"Yes, diaper, leave a few just in case," said War Plane. He watched Clifton as the little boy rested Baby Tiffany in Peaches' arms. After Clifton gave the baby to Peaches, he walked to the dresser and pulled out one of its lower drawers. He removed the pack of diapers that he had bought at the shop the day before. He took three diapers out of the pack and laid them beside a pillow next to Peaches' head.

Peaches looked around at the hundreds of large orange-and-brown paper wasps on the bed beside her and hugged Baby Tiffany close to her chest. She started to regret that she hadn't stopped Lanky Roy from carrying the mongrel dog to the river the day before. She turned to Clifton. "Hey, Cliffy, mi sweet nephew. A swear a never know that Lanky was going to dash you pet dog in the river. Him tell mi that him was only going to set the dog on the riverbank to tempt the crocodile."

"Well," said Clifton, "you tell him to test if the cage them work last night. You encourage him to capture the sick puss."

Peaches looked like she was about to burst out in tears. "No, a was planning on telling him—"

"The only thing you did a plan to do, a how to spend the stray animal cleanup money."

Peaches took out the five thousand dollars from between her bosoms and held it out to Clifton. "See the money here, mi nephew, you can buy anything you want."

Clifton looked at the money in her hand, shook his head, and walked away from the bed, leaving her looking at him.

War Plane flew off the dresser and landed on Clifton's shoulder once more and said something to him. Clifton nodded his head with a smile and walked toward the kitchen. War Plane flew off his shoulder and flew into the kitchen.

*   *   *

Inside the kitchen, Clifton saw Lanky Roy and Yabba whispering to each other. Yabba had come out of his tablecloth cocoon and was standing close to Lanky Roy beside the dining table. He was holding on to his fat and shiny top lip. War Plane, Chicken Hawk, and No-Shame were standing on the kitchen counter, observing the two pathetic humans.

"Okay, Lanky," said Clifton, "the Animal Committee want you and Yabba to meet them at the riverside now. You have less than ten minutes."

Lanky Roy could not fathom why the animals wanted him and Yabba at the riverside. From what he had witnessed so far, he knew that it was an order and not a suggestion. He looked at Yabba for help, but Yabba was looking confused.

Lanky Roy turned to Clifton. "Okay," he said, scratching his head. "Just open the back door so mi and Yabba can run to the river—"

"No, Lanky," said Clifton, "you can't run or drive to the river, you can't stop and talk to anybody either. You and Yabba have to walk behind each other like two prisoners."

Lanky Roy started to argue, but Clifton pushed him hard toward the door. Lanky Roy lifted a hand to hit Clifton.

At the same time, one of the wasps flew off the stove and stung Lanky Roy on his hand before he could hit the boy. Lanky Roy cried out in pain and held his hand. Clifton removed the key from his pants pocket and opened the kitchen back door.

The three humans stepped outside in the heat of the hot sun. Clifton shielded his eyes and looked up at the sky, where he saw that the sun was almost in the middle of the sky. Several John Crows were flying high overhead but low enough to warn Lanky Roy and Yabba that the Animal Committee meant business.

Stinger and his security crew were still resting on the outside wall of the house. They all flew off the wall and circled a few feet over the two animal abusers' head.

War Plane, Chicken Hawk, and No-Shame flew out of the kitchen and landed on the clothesline.

No-Shame used his beak to pull off a piece of paper napkin that was stuck to the bottom of one of his feet. "You not telling Clifton to lock the back door, War Plane, suppose Peaches escape?" he asked.

"That is why the wasp them is guarding her, No-Shame," said Chicken Hawk. "Them making sure she can't call for human help before we get to the river with them two wicked brute here."

"Ohh, a see," said No-Shame, trying to flick the piece of paper napkin that had gotten wedged in his beak.

"As soon as we reach the river, all the wasps is supposed to leave," said War Plane, looking at No-Shame with the piece of napkin in his beak. "The Animal Committee don't care what she do after we reach the river."

"So, how mi going know when you all reach the river?" asked No- Shame. He sounded funny talking with the piece of napkin in his beak.

"It shouldn't take we more than five minutes to reach the river," said Chicken Hawk.

"Okay then," said No-Shame, "a will give you six minutes before a leave."

"Before you leave go where?" asked War Plane.

"To the riverside," said No-Shame. "You say, once you all reach the river, the Committee don't care—"

"No, man," said War Plane, "you is supposed to stay and guard the outside of the house, just in case Miss Bleaching Cream escape . . . she can't, but is Billy G orders."

No-Shame shifted uncomfortably on the clothesline.

He didn't like the fact that he was about to be left out of what was going to take place at the riverside. He didn't like his job in the operation; he didn't sign on for any security-bird job. He was there to intimidate the humans, and that's what he wanted to do. The only thing he felt he had done so far was to destroy an innocent pot of food. "So what if she call for help after the wasps leave?" he asked.

"The first sign of humans, you is supposed to call down the entire John Crow battalion overhead on the housetop. We just doing that as fun."

"Yes," said Clifton, "just as how them throw Mongrel in the water yester-day to the crocodile for fun."

"Ohh-kaay," said No-Shame, turning to War Plane. "A get the idea now, brothers-in-arms . . . Pechary and John Crow teamwork."

War Plane ignored No-Shame's enthusiasm and looked at Lanky Roy and Yabba, who were both covering their heads with their two hands. They were protecting their heads because Stinger and his thugs continued to circle them.

War Plane shifted on the clothesline so he could get closer to Clifton. "Check if one of them fools here have a cell phone on them," he said.

"Cell phone?" asked Clifton.

"Just do it, is Billy G want it," said War Plane.

Clifton patted all the pockets of Lanky Roy's and Yabba's clothing until he found a Razr cell phone in one of the pockets of Yabba's jeans. He flipped it open and saw that the screen was not giving off any light.

"Look like the battery dead, mon, mi forget to charge it last night," said Yabba.

Clifton returned the cell phone to Yabba's pocket and told War Plane to give him a minute. He limped off in the house and returned shortly with Peaches' iPhone. He showed it to War Plane, who was looking pleased that

Clifton had found a working phone.

Clifton pushed the cell phone in his pants pocket. "Okay, a guess we can leave now," he said while wondering why Billy G needed a cell phone.

Chicken Hawk flew off the clothesline and soared a few feet over Lanky Roy's and Yabba's heads. "Yes, them two wicked brute here due at the riverside any moment now."

"Hold on," said War Plane, turning to Clifton, "we going need a long piece a rope. Lanky Roy have any here?"

Clifton nodded and hobbled into the laundry room. He returned with the piece of rope that was behind the door. It was about fifteen feet long. He folded the rope in two and then hung it over one of his shoulders. He looked at Lanky Roy and Yabba and noticed that both men were sweating profusely in the hot sun. "Move up, walk to the gate in a single file," he said.

Yabba quickly moved ahead of Lanky Roy because he wanted to be in front. He didn't want to look ridiculous, walking closely behind Lanky Roy in the middle of the road. He also didn't like the fact that Clifton had that long piece of rope. He was sure it wasn't for a game of skipping or to make a tree swing. He knew that rope was for something sinister, and that made him wish he had followed his mind and turned down Lanky Roy's job offer. He walked on while he thought about what was going to happen at the riverside.

When they reached the front of the yard, Lanky Roy looked toward the doghouse to see if Putus would be awake to bark or even growl at the kidnapping birds. Lanky Roy was shocked to see Putus's silver chain lying on the ground. One end of the chain was still attached to the doghouse, but the other end was not attached to Putus. The huge Rottweiler was not there. Lanky Roy could not believe his eyes; his expensive dog was missing. He wondered if Putus's disappearance and the cat getting out of the cage were connected. He kept his thought to himself and followed closely behind Yabba.

When they were close to the gate, War Plane called out to Clifton. "Stop them, both of them," he said. Clifton did what he was told, and both men stopped.

Lanky Roy was worried; he knew that something was not right. He didn't see a reason for Clifton to stop them because he felt that he and Yabba were both cooperating to the fullest of their ability.

War Plane flew in front of Clifton's face and gave him another instruction for both men to do. Clifton chuckled to himself as he listened to War Plane's instructions.

After War Plane finished with his instructions, Clifton said to both men, "Okay, the two of you, take off you footwear," he said, "both shoes and slippers."

Lanky Roy stopped and turned to Clifton. "You mad, you don't feel how the sun hot?" he asked. "The road supposed to be boiling—"

"Just take off you slippers," said Clifton, "before a tell the pechary to inform the wasps that you ignoring orders."

Lanky Roy looked at Yabba, who was already barefoot.

Yabba was out of his shoe before Clifton had finished instructing them. He wasn't taking any chances; he couldn't take another wasp sting. If the birds wanted him to strip and dance in the middle of the road, he would have done it. He looked at Lanky Roy, who was hesitating to take off his flip-flops. "Take off the rahtid slippers, Lanky Roy, mon," he said.

Lanky Roy looked up at the swarm of wasp circling over his and Yabba's head and began to remove his slippers.

Clifton felt like a grown man; he couldn't believe what was happening. He was ordering his abusive uncle around the same way his uncle used to do to him. He pinched himself on the arm to see if he was dreaming. He never knew he would live to see that day. He watched as Lanky Roy removed his last slipper and threw it down beside the other slipper on the ground. "All right, now the two of you walk in a single file to the gate," he ordered.

Both men obeyed Clifton and walked to the gate. When they reached the gate, Yabba pushed it open. He and Lanky Roy reluctantly walked through the gate as if they were afraid to venture out of the yard. They started to take baby steps on a soft patch of grass that led from the gate to the road.

While cautiously tiptoeing, Lanky Roy looked at the flat tires on the car at the gate. The sight of the punctured tires was even more frightening in the day. He was convinced that it was not Pickah, the cokehead, who had punctured the tires. The animals, birds, and insects seemed to be working as a team to punish him and Yabba. Even though he didn't want to admit it to himself, he was starting to feel scared.

A deep guttural growl coming from across the road caught Lanky Roy's attention. He looked across the road and saw two of the menacing mongrel dogs from the Hungry Belly Crew standing and looking at him and Yabba. The other member of the crew emerged from behind the car. All three dogs moved in close to the two cruel humans and started to growl and snarl at them with their sharp jagged teeth. Lanky Roy held on to his throbbing wasp-stung hand and hurried behind Yabba while looking at the angry dogs from the corner of his eyes.

When they reached the end of the patch of grass, Lanky Roy and Yabba stopped walking. Both men looked at their bare feet and looked at the road. The sun was so hot; they could see the heat waves dancing off the gritty asphalt road.

Clifton shoved Lanky Roy hard in the middle of his back, and the lanky man pitched forward and knocked both himself and Yabba onto the hot road.

Yabba jumped about three feet in the air as soon as his bare feet touched the road's hot surface. The hot and sharp, tiny pebbles on the road maximized his pain and discomfort.

Lanky Roy couldn't bear the heat. The bare soles of his feet felt like they were on a hot barbecue grill. In order to keep his feet off the scorched road, he began to lift both of his feet off the ground one after another like a young soldier learning to march. He looked around to see if any of his neighbors were around to help him and Yabba, but everyone was in their house, sheltered from the hot midday sun.

Clifton looked at Lanky Roy and Yabba as they knitted their brows and gritted their teeth in order to bear the pain caused by the hot road. He was enjoying every bit of the men's discomfort. "Run," he said to both men, "the pechary say you can run to the river now."

Anxious to get off the fiery road, both men gladly ran in the direction of the shortcut that led to the river. The three members of the Hungry Belly Crew ran behind them. Clifton looked around for Sufferer, but the mangy old dog was nowhere in sight. He took the piece of rope off his shoulder, held it in his hand, and started to run so that he could keep up with Lanky Roy and Yabba. While running, he smiled and looked at the men running to the riverside where they would meet their Waterloo.

CHAPTER SIXTEEN

The heat from the hot sun scorched the riverbank below. The riverside was as silent as a ghost town. The branches of the trees along the riverbank barely moved as the wind seemed to disappear from among them. Even the murky water of the Rio Cobre looked like glass as it moved lazily downstream. The human footprints from the day before had formed into hardened molds along the river's bank. Mongrel and Putus lay beside each other under the avocado tree. They watched as Stinger and his swarm of security thugs led Lanky Roy and Yabba toward the river. The three mongrel dogs from the Hungry Belly Crew were on their heels. Clifton ran behind both men, while War Plane and Chicken Hawk flew a few feet over their heads.

When Clifton and the others reached the riverside, Clifton saw Mongrel and Putus sitting under the avocado tree. He ran to the mongrel dog and fell to his knees. He hugged the dog and kissed its head. Clifton felt like he had won the lottery; it was the most wonderful feeling he ever had in his life. Mongrel was also happy to see his one and only human friend. He licked Clifton's face and rested his head on the boy's right shoulder.

Lanky Roy walked over to Putus and tried to rub the dog's head, but the large Rottweiler snapped and barked at him. Lanky Roy pulled his hands away and looked at Yabba with disbelief.

Yabba stepped close to Lanky Roy and whispered. "This serious, Lanky, this no look good."

Lanky Roy gave Yabba a slight nod, but his mind was preoccupied. He was thinking of a way to escape the deadly wasps that were circling above their heads.

Lanky Roy's thinking was cut short by sounds coming from some of the bushes on the riverbank. He, Yabba, and Clifton looked toward the bushes, where they saw the rest of the animals walking out from some of the bushes that grew on the riverbank. Most of the animals started to converge under the avocado tree.

The birds flew out of various treetops that they were hiding in. They landed on the ground and on nearby tree branches.

The three mongrel dogs from the Hungry Belly Crew, Ras Blah Blah, Grunty, the two teenage ram goats, and the Red Poll bull from the meeting walked to Lanky Roy and Yabba. They all made a huge circle around the two humans.

Bruck Kitchen was on the highest limb of the avocado tree. He held on tight to a tree branch. Not even a category-five hurricane could get him out of the tree. He was making sure that Lanky Roy was in no position to harm him before he climbed down.

Earlier on in the day, Grunty had told Bruck Kitchen that he had seen the puny-looking cat that had escaped from Lanky Roy's laundry room. The cat told the fat pig that it was counting its lucky stars and was not coming to the riverbank because Lanky Roy and Yabba were going to be there. Bruck Kitchen had supported the cat's decision 100 percent.

The two Kling Kling blackbirds from Manchester were perched on a limb of the avocado tree. Billy G had told them to stand back and watch how the event was going to unfold. He had decided not to get them involved because they were visitors.

Doc, the doctor bird, had gotten scared and decided to be an observer rather than a partaker. He was observing from a limb of the calabash tree that was close to the avocado tree.

Muliesha, the mule, had sent a message to Billy G that she had a terrible toothache, so she had to stay home. The wise billy goat didn't buy the female mule's excuse, but he didn't have time to voice his opinion on that.

None of the animals or birds had seen Sufferer since the announcement that Lanky Roy and Yabba were capturing stray animals. It was rumored that the mangy old dog had migrated to a nearby community. There were other rumors that he had started the long journey to the nearest animal shelter in Kingston. No one could confirm the rumors, and Kas Kas was very happy that no one could blame her because she had promised to refrain from her rumor-spreading ways. She had chosen to stay out of trouble and watch from the top of the calabash tree.

Jacko, the spider, was relaxing on a lower limb of the avocado tree. He felt that because he had planned some of the retaliation strategies, it was the other animals' and birds' duty to put it into effect.

Nanny Stush watched cowardly from behind a lime tree. Hebrew stood beside her, praying to God to forgive the Animal Committee for what they were about to do to the two adult male humans. Jenny was on Hebrew's back, trying to tell the Christian donkey that the Animal Committee was only doing what it thought was best for the animals' and birds' future.

Lorna was resting under the lime tree. She was tired, but she was also curious to see what the Animal Committee was going to do at the riverside.

White Squall, the gawling bird that had tall legs and white feathers, was perched in a tall tree close to the main road to look out for any humans who looked like they were going to the river.

The large swarm of wasps that was left behind in Peaches' bedroom flew from the direction of the shortcut and flew toward the rest of the wasps that were circling over Yabba's and Lanky Roy's heads. Yabba's two knees gave way when he saw the large swarm of wasp approaching the riverside. The very sight of the wasps was enough to scare him to death. He dropped to his knees, shielded his head with one hand, and used the other hand to cover his swollen lip.

Clifton stood back and watched as Billy G walked out of a thick bunch of cuscus grass and stopped beside the group of animals that had surrounded Lanky Roy and Yabba. "Eh ehm," he said, clearing his throat and looking at the crowd. "Gentle peeps, today, we're going to show the humans that we animals—and the birds too—are not a bunch of pushovers."

He made one of his famous dramatic pauses to let his words sink in among the rest of his folks. They all nodded in agreement. Even Hebrew nodded her head before she realized what she was doing. She stopped and looked if Nanny Stush had seen her nodding, then closed her one good eye and started to pray again.

Billy G looked up at Stinger, the leader of the wasp community. "Stinger, no humans can see beneath the pear tree from the top of the road, so get them under it until we are ready for them."

Stinger obeyed the wise old billy goat and ordered his thugs to fly closer to both men. The wasp thugs converged and dived toward Yabba's and Lanky Roy's upper bodies. Both of the animal abusers stepped back until they were directly beneath the avocado tree. The animals that had surrounded them moved under the tree as well.

Billy G walked to Clifton and stopped in front of him. "Welcome, my one and only human friend," he said, tilting his head back to adjust the old eyeglass frame on his nose. "Did War Plane tell you to carry a cell phone?"

Clifton nodded and took out Peaches' iPhone and showed it to the old goat.

Billy G smiled at Clifton. "Good. I want you to—"

"Is a iPhone Peaches own?" asked Jacko, climbing down out of the tree.

"A can bet you, it don't have no credit on it—"

"Ahhhh!" screamed Guana, the green lizard who was resting on the trunk of the avocado tree. "You step on mi tail, man."

Jacko looked at Guana's tail. "Sorry, man, a never see you."

"Is because a change color for the mission," said Guana. "A blend in with the color of the tree bark just in case Billy G want a surprise attack."

"Oh yeah?" asked Jacko. "A blend you blend in with the tree bark so you can hide . . . a coward, you coward."

"Look here, don't get on mi nerves today, you think is Jenny this—"

"Knock it off, guys!" shouted Billy G, looking at Jacko over the rim of the old eyeglass. "Now is definitely not the time or place." Even though Jacko had interrupted him, it reminded the wise old goat that he had forgotten to tell War Plane to let the boy check if credit was on the phone. He turned to Clifton. "Check the credit. If no minutes are not on it, we will have to resort to plan B, hopefully we don't have to."

Lanky Roy looked at Clifton using the cell phone and wondered what was going to happen. He looked toward the main road and thought about making a run for it, but the large swarm of wasps that had joined Stinger and his thugs were monitoring his and Yabba's every move. He was even afraid to scratch his nose. He decided he just had to stay put and hope for the best.

Clifton disconnected the call and turned to the president of the Animal Committee. "Okay, she have ninety dollars on it."

"Good, that means we are in business," said Billy G. "Dial 114 for the operator and ask for the phone number for the TV station that was here yesterday—"

"And tell them what?" asked Clifton.

"Tell them that you see two male lovers about to commit suicide by jumping in the Rio Cobre River."

"O Jesus," said Hebrew, praying faster.

"Suicide and male lovers?" asked Grunty, the pig. "What kinda Jerry Springer story that, Billy G?"

Some of the animals and birds shared Grunty's concern by looking at Billy G.

"Relax, Grunty," said Jacko, "what him should tell them that him see a group a animals have two humans hostage?"

Billy G looked at the animals and birds. "Gentle peeps, if I let Clifton tell them the truth, they would laugh at him," he said, "but when they hear a story like what Clifton is about to feed them, they will reach out here faster than how they were born."

A few of them nodded their heads as they all waited in suspense for Clifton to get off the phone. Clifton signaled for them to keep quiet as he spoke with someone from the television newsroom. Clifton stayed on the cell phone for about a minute and a half and then got off with a broad smile on his face. He gave them the news they were all waiting for. "Is a lady, she sound happy," he said. "She say one a them news team will be here in less than ten minutes."

Billy G pumped a hoof in the air. "Yes, let the lesson begin!" He turned to Stinger and the animals that were keeping both men hostage. "Move them close to the edge of the river—more downriver though—no one can see that part of the river from the main road."

Clifton told both men to walk closer to the river.

It was the first time Yabba hesitated to follow Clifton's instruction. He did not like the move-closer-to-the-river order. He started to have a bad feeling in his stomach. He and Lanky Roy walked downriver and stopped about eight feet from the edge of the river.

Ras Blah Blah, Grunty, and the rest of the animals who were guarding the men followed them while maintaining the circle around them.

The large swarm of wasps continued to circle the men's head. Some of them flew to the dirt road that led to the main road and hovered over it. They didn't want Lanky Roy and Yabba to use it as an escape route.

Billy G looked around to see if any other humans were around, but no other humans were in sight. He turned to Clifton. "Tell them to sit down. Don't let them face each other. I want them back-to-back."

Clifton repeated the instruction to both men. Yabba sat down with his face to the river, and Lanky Roy with his face to the main road.

Billy G took a step to Clifton. "Now, use the rope you have in your hand," he said, "and wrap it around their waist and leave a long end about eight feet."

All the animals and birds drew closer and watched Clifton while he wrapped the long piece of rope several times around Lanky Roy's and Yabba's chests. Each time Clifton wrapped the rope around the men, he made a nonslip knot. Both men tried to wriggle out of the rope, but Stinger and his thugs flew closer to them. With the dangerous wasps flying so close to their heads, both men relaxed and cooperated with their captors.

The animals and birds looked on in astonishment. They didn't know that Billy G and the Animal Committee were going to take it to that level, but they were enjoying the look of fear on Lanky Roy's and Yabba's faces.

After Clifton finished binding the men, he gave the rope a final tie and let a long piece of it dangle to the ground. He looked at the wise billy goat for further instruction.

As Billy G was about to say something, Ras Blah Blah, the Rasta sheep, walked up to him. "It's a pity we never have a chain instead of a rope because Babylon bound we with chains over the years, but the rope will do."

Billy G held a hoof up at the Rasta sheep. "Okay, Ras, a hear you." He looked at the Red Poll bull from the meeting and pointed his right hoof at him. "Bucka T, grab the end of the rope." Bucka T quickly swallowed a wad of cud and picked up the rope with his mouth. Billy G then turned to Mongrel. "Mongrel, you hold on to the rope too, just a few feet below Bucka T."

Mongrel walked up to the rope and used his rickety teeth to hold on to his part of the rope.

With a baffled look on his face, Grunty approached Billy G. "Billy, tell mi something, why you never let mi hold part a the rope?"

"You're not strong enough, Grunty. Bucka T is a bull. Bulls have stronger jawbones than pigs."

"I agree with that," said Grunty, "but Mongrel jawbone no stronger than mine."

"I know, but the only reason I use Mongrel," said Billy G, looking at the captured humans, "is because I want Lanky Roy and Yabba to learn that they must do unto others as they would like others do unto them."

"Fair enough," said Grunty, stepping back to watch the scenario.

After Billy G saw that Bucka T and Mongrel had their part of rope secured in their mouth, he walked to Clifton and whispered something to the boy.

Clifton looked at Lanky Roy and Yabba. The men looked like they were about to defecate. Clifton smiled and walked up to Lanky Roy. He stooped with his face close to his uncle's face. "Um, Lanky," he said, "Billy G say this is call turn-back blow. Him say it mean, when a person do wickedness in life, wickedness it can turn back on them." He stood up and looked at Billy G with a triumphant grin on his face.

Billy G walked to the very edge of the riverbank. "Okay, gentle peeps, victory is near." He looked up at the tree where White Squall was watching and called out to him. "Hey, Squall! Everything good?" he asked.

White Squall lifted a wing. "Yes, just one and two car passing, but no sign of any human walking to the river!"

"Okay, sounds good!" shouted Billy G. He turned to Mongrel and Bucka T. "Pull them in the river now."

Mongrel began to pull with all his might, but he could feel Bucka T pulling him and both humans toward the river with his strong jawbones.

Lanky Roy started to pull away from the river, but Putus moved in and started to bark at him. The menacing mongrel dogs from the Hungry Belly Crew joined Putus and began to snarl, growl, and bite at his and Yabba's feet.

For the first time, Lanky Roy wished he had listened to Yabba. The animals and birds were executing their revenge, and it was too late for him to do something about it.

Both of the animal abusers were a few inches away from the river when Yabba looked in the murky river. In the water, he saw a large crocodile waiting for them. The crocodile was much larger than the one that he and Lanky Roy had tried to feed Mongrel to the day before. The crocodile opened its huge mouth as Mongrel, and Bucka T pulled him and Lanky Roy closer to the river.

Yabba looked in the gaping mouth of the crocodile and screamed at the top of his lungs. "Whoooiiii, mi dead . . . we dead. Lanky, mi and you dead now!" he bawled. A dark spot began to form below the zipper of his blue jeans.

Seeing the horror that was about to take place, Hebrew kneeled on her two front legs, causing Jenny, who was on her back to fall off.

Jenny landed on the top of her head, but she quickly got up and looked at Hebrew. "Hebrew, what the hell get into you?"

Hebrew didn't hear a single word that Jenny had said because she was too busy praying. Her two front knees were clasped tight beneath her chin, and her face was raised to the sky. "Lord, forgive Billy G and the rest of the committee 'cause they don't know what they have done," she said.

Bruck Kitchen, the thieving cat, saw that Lanky Roy was in no position to hurt him. He quickly climbed down the tree and ran to the riverbank and stopped beside Grunty. "Yow, Grunty," he said, "Lanky Roy can't shoot mi with him slingshot again because—"

Screech! The screeching sound of car tires was heard coming from the main road. All the animals and birds looked toward the main road. The ones that were on the ground couldn't see the vehicle from where they were, but they could hear the opening and slamming of its doors.

Billy G turned to them. "Bush it, bush it, gentle peeps!" he shouted. He and some of the animals and birds ran and hid in a thick clump of bush upriver. The two Kling Kling blackbirds flew out of the avocado tree and flew in the bushes with them.

Doc hid in the calabash tree he was sitting in.

Grunty darted off downriver. "A what wrong with Squall, man?" he asked while sprinting.

Mongrel and Bucka T dropped the rope from out of their mouths and ran away from Lanky Roy and Yabba. They stopped a few yards farther downriver beside Putus, who was pretending to drink water by the animals' regular drinking-spot.

Some of the other animals, including Ras Blah Blah, scampered off behind some trees upriver.

Stinger and the entire swarm of wasp flew to the opposite side of the river and landed on the trunk of a dead tree.

Jenny pecked Hebrew on her back with her beak to get her attention. "Take you bag a bone self up and run!" she shouted. She ran off upriver.

Hebrew quickly got to her feet and ran after Jenny.

"Oh my god, wait for me!" shouted Nanny Stush, jogging daintily behind them.

Lorna could hardly move. She scrambled to her feet and ran behind Nanny Stush with her swollen belly swinging beneath her.

Bruck Kitchen had run back to the avocado tree faster than how he had come down.

Jacko was already sitting on the tallest limb of the tree, watching the chaos happening below.

Guana, who had turned fully dark brown, mistakenly jumped off the tree and landed on a piece of white paper that was blown from the main road and ended up under the tree.

From the top of the tree, Jacko spotted Guana on the piece of white paper below and called out to him. "Wrong background, Guana!"

Guana looked down on the piece of white paper he had landed on and jumped off it. He shot up in the avocado tree and hid on one of its dry brown twigs.

Clifton took up a few stones and began to throw one of the stones at a large green avocado that was hanging from one of the avocado tree's lower limbs.

*　　*　　*

High up in the treetop close to the main road, White Squall was shifting from one foot to the other. He was worrying that Billy G was going to have his head on a platter because he didn't spot the human vehicle in time. He swore there was no vehicle in sight. It was as if the vehicle had appeared out of thin air. He tried to relax as he continued to watch the pandemonium at the riverside.

*　　*　　*

Lanky Roy and Yabba struggled to stand up on their feet. Lanky Roy watched as a female reporter and a cameraman ran down the dirt road toward them. A few curious onlookers, who had seen the television news vehicle, had gotten out of their vehicles and were following the news team down the dirt road.

The cameraman ran to the edge of the river with his camera on his shoulder and began to videotape both men.

The female reporter looked at Lanky Roy and Yabba and then walked over to Clifton. She started to question him. "Excuse me," she said, "are you the person who called the newsroom about two men trying to kill themselves?"

"Yes, miss, them over there," said Clifton, pointing at Lanky Roy and Yabba who, had managed to partially work themselves out of the rope that was around their chest. "Best friends trying to kill them self together."

The news reporter looked toward Lanky Roy and Yabba. "Best friends? A thought you said they were two love—never mind," she said, looking back at Clifton. "Why would they want to kill themselves?"

"Debbie," said the cameraman, pointing to Yabba and Lanky Roy. "Let me get you asking them that question."

The female reporter laughed and walked to the cameraman. She handed him the end of a microphone cable that she had in her hand. "Sorry, a got carried away with the lovers' story," she said. "Look like a prank call to me."

The cameraman took the end of the cable that had an input plug and inserted it in the back of his video camera. "Prank call?" he asked, looking at Lanky Roy and Yabba. "Then how them two man here tie up together like scallion and thyme so?"

"Well, that's what we going find out now," said the reporter, brushing back her hair with her free hand. "You ready?" she asked.

"Give me a sec," said the cameraman. He lifted the heavy video camera onto his right shoulder, held up his left hand, and began to countdown silently with three fingers.

Debbie cleared her throat and looked into the camera's lens. "We are here at Iron Bridge, a small community in Saint Catherine. We are at a section of the community that runs along the Rio Cobre River. Upon arrival, we saw two men bound with a rope at the edge of the river. Both men were seen in a kneeling position. I am about to speak to the men to get a full understanding of what is going on." She walked toward Lanky Roy and Yabba, who had successfully freed each other from the bondage of the rope. They both had dirt all over their clothes.

Yabba saw the reporter walking to him and Lanky Roy and covered the wet spot at the front of his jeans with his hands.

Lanky Roy removed the last of the rope from around his chest and threw it on the ground. The reporter walked to him and held the mike close to his face. "Sir, can you explain what is going on here?"

Lanky Roy pointed at Clifton. "Lady, that wicked nephew a have over there bring mi and mi friend here against our will."

"I don't understand. How can a little boy tie up two grown men, sir?"

"No, him get help, ma'am. See, all them animal around you that acting like them drinking water?" said Lanky Roy, pointing to Bucka T, Mongrel, and Putus drinking water at the riverside. "All a them plan up to feed we to the crocodile."

"What crocodile?" asked the reporter.

Yabba pointed at the river, but the crocodile was no longer in the water. "Um . . . a big fat crocodile was in the water, miss, and that bull cow and mongrel dog try to feed we to it."

The reporter tried to hide a smirk as she listened to Yabba's story.

"Is true him talking, ma'am," said Lanky Roy, trying to convince the news reporter that they were telling the truth. "A big crocodile was in the water. Three birds capture we and bring we to the river, and the leader who is a goat order that dog and bull cow to drag we to the river."

The news reporter waved a hand at Bucka T, Mongrel, and Putus. "So you are saying those stray animals captured both of you from your homes—"

"No, miss," said Yabba, shaking his head. "A was over his yard when the three birds kidnapped we."

There was hushed laughter from a small group of spectators that were watching the interview. "It look like them is two cokeheads," said one of the spectators.

"Okaay," said the reporter. She wanted to laugh, but she had to keep it professional. "But why would the birds and animals want to capture you and feed you to a crocodile?"

Yabba was getting annoyed that the reporter didn't believe them, so he decided he was going to tell her the truth. "Well, miss, what happen is, yesterday at the river—owhch!"

Lanky Roy nudged Yabba in the rib with an elbow. "Him talking foolishness, miss, the thing is—"

"Don't move, you two are under arrest," said a voice that was coming from the direction of the main road. They all looked and saw two policemen walking down the dirt road toward them. One of the policemen was skinny, and the other was fat. Lanky Roy and Yabba were too busy trying to convince the reporter that they didn't notice the two policemen.

Yabba tried to run, but his knees failed him once more. He fell to the ground with his hands and knees in the dirt.

The fat policeman walked to Yabba and pulled him to his feet. He put both of Yabba's hands behind his back and snapped on a pair of shiny handcuffs on his wrists.

Lanky Roy was too shocked to move; it was as if every muscle in his body was out of service. He just stood there while the skinny policeman handcuffed him.

"Excuse me, Officer," said the reporter to the fat policeman who was holding on to Yabba. "What are these two men being arrested for?"

The fat policeman pointed at Yabba. "We arresting this man for cruelty to a dumb animal, and the other one," he said, pointing to Lanky Roy, "is for the same thing, but we arresting him for child abuse too."

"Okay, so how does that tie in with the animal cruelty, can you explain that?"

"A can't say much, but what a can say is, we have evidence to support both arrest. That's all a can say at the moment."

Suddenly, there was a shout of joy coming from Clifton. They all turned to see him limping off to meet a short and stocky dark-skinned lady who was walking down the dirt road that led from the main road. "Mommy!" he said, hugging the lady around her waist. The lady kissed Clifton on both of his cheeks.

Lanky Roy looked at the lady with his mouth wide open. He was shocked and surprised to see her. He didn't know that his sister was coming to Jamaica. Her sudden appearance had caught him off guard. His sister walked up to him and looked at him with disdain in her eyes.

"How dare you take ma money and treat ma child like that?" she asked. "You don't think a have good friends live in Jamaica, worthless bwoy?"

Lanky Roy was so ashamed that he couldn't look his sister in the eye. He just stood there, looking down at the dry riverbank.

The news reporter approached Lanky Roy's sister and held the microphone to her face. "Excuse me, miss, are you the mother of this child?"

"Yes, am his mother," said the lady, pulling Clifton closer to her. "For eight years, a working in the United States and sending money for ma son and not a dollar was spend on him." She pointed at Clifton's feet. "Look at the ole shoes ma pickney have on."

Lanky Roy couldn't stand the embarrassment any longer; he lifted up his head and looked at his sister. "Joyce, mi sorry—"

"A don't want any sorry from you, Lanky," said Joyce. "After you come out from jail, a want you out of ma house that a paying rent for. Both you and you worthless baby mother. And I done talk." She turned to the skinny policeman who was holding Lanky Roy. "Mr. Officer, move him from in front of ma face." She looked at Lanky Roy. "And a need ma car key. A hear ma brand-new car look like a rat nest."

"The car key on top a the fridge," said Lanky Roy. He felt like he wanted to cry. He couldn't believe he was that stupid to make the decisions that he had made during the last twenty-four hours. He wished he had gone to look for a job rather than depending on his sister's income. He started to blame Peaches in his mind. He felt that if she were a good woman, she would've insisted that he not take Speng Shell's offer instead of pocketing the five thousand dollars. He silently cursed Yabba too, but he knew deep down in his heart that he was the only person who was to blame. He felt like he wanted to run and drown himself in the river. He wanted to beg the malnourished policeman who was holding him to throw him in the river. He struggled to hold back the tears that had started to trickle from his eyes, but he couldn't. He burst out in tears as his sister, nephew, and everyone around him looked at him.

The spectators began to laugh at Lanky Roy's crying.

Both policemen had a smug look on their faces. They were purposefully lingering so that the cameraman could capture Lanky Roy's embarrassing moment. After they were satisfied, they led both Lanky Roy and Yabba toward a police car that was parked on the main road.

The news reporter turned to the camera lens and began to wrap up her report. The group of spectators started to make their way to the main road. Some of them smiled at Joyce as they walked past her.

Joyce returned a friendly smile at the spectators. She looked at Clifton and gently rubbed the long scar on the left side of his head. "Don't worry, ma son, mommy is here to take care of you, okay. Come on, a still remember the shortcut. Let's go home."

Joyce and her son began to walk to the shortcut when the ringing of a BlackBerry cell phone, which she had in her hand, interrupted her. She stopped walking, looked at the cell phone's screen, and answered the incoming call.

"Hi, what's up?" she said. She listened while she made a big nod. "Good, make her go on. Good for her and me too, thank God. Yes, thanks for the information." She hung up the phone and turned to Clifton.

"Is what?" asked Clifton.

"That was Mass Gilbert next door. Him say Peaches is moving out her clothes and belongings out of the house into a taxi. She probably going back to her mother in Kingston."

Clifton looked to the ground and sighed heavily. "Well, a going miss cousin Tiffy, but a not going miss Peaches," he said. He removed Peaches' iPhone out of his pants pocket and showed it to his mother. "A have her phone, Mommy."

Joyce put her two hands akimbo and gave her son a suspicious look. "What you doing with her cellphone?"

Clifton's mind raced as he thought of an answer to his mother's question. "The animals tell mi to . . . a mean a tell mi self that because Uncle Lanky wicked to mi and the dog, a would use it and call the police."

Joyce patted her son his shoulder. "Good thinking, ma son, a proud of you. That is why a never tell anybody a coming. A come and went straight to the police station. Thank God for Mass Gilbert."

Clifton did a sigh of relief. He realized that he had almost mistakenly told his mother that it was the animals that had ordered the use of the cell phone. He wondered how she would have taken that explanation if he hadn't caught himself in time. "Yeah, a glad you come home, Mommy."

"Me too, son. Come on, let us go home," said Joyce. "Ma taxi friend a charter, probably reach the house with ma luggage. A tell him to drop me at the station then meet me at the house after."

Clifton looked around; all the spectators had left. Only he, his mother, and the news team were left on the riverside. The news reporter and the cameraman walked to his and his mother's direction. "Hold on, Mommy," he said. He hobbled off to Bucka T, Mongrel, and Putus, who were still at the riverside pretending to drink water. When Clifton got there, he kneeled and hugged Mongrel. "Come on, we going home, Mongrel. No more Lanky Roy and Peaches to bother we."

Mongrel lifted his head to the sky. "Thank God, a can't wait to get a good meal," he said. He looked to Putus and Bucka T. They all nodded their heads in approval for him to go home with his human friend.

"Go on, leave mi," said Putus. "A tired a the chain and that doghouse. A staying to experience life at the Fruit Basket."

"You sure?" asked Clifton. He looked around at his mother to see if she had noticed that he was talking to the animals, but his mother was busy talking to the news team.

"Yes, a sure," said Putus. "You and Mongrel go home. Home is where both of you heart is. Mine is to explore the area. See you around."

"Okay, cool," said Clifton. "A just want to know you sure about that." He looked at Mongrel. "Come, Mong, let's go home sweet home."

"Hold on a bit, Clif," said Mongrel, looking at the huge Rottweiler. "Thanks for the advice, Putus."

"No problem." Putus smiled. "I know you love you yard; that's why I said you must go home."

"Yeah, man," said Mongrel, turning to Bucka T. "And thank for the love and support you all show mi, Buck."

"No problem Mong," said the Red Poll bull. "That's what the committee is here for."

"Hey, Mongrel," said Putus, stepping close to the mongrel dog. "Thanks for not showing mi any bad face when Lanky Roy put mi before you. If it was some dog, they would try harm mi in mi sleep."

"You welcome, Putus," said Mongrel. "As Ras Blah Blah once say at a meeting, it no make sense you jealous someone because jealousy bring forth hatred, and hatred will destroy you life."

They all nodded their heads at the Rasta sheep's quoted speech. Clifton stood up and looked around. Knowing that most of the animals who were hiding could see him from their hiding places, he silently mouthed the words "Love you all." He then turned around and limped off to his mother, who was still talking to the news team. Mongrel followed behind him, happily wagging his tail.

All the animals and birds watched Clifton, and his mother waved goodbye to the news people. Both mother and son turned and walked in the direction of the shortcut. Mongrel ran beside them while jumping and bouncing in the air.

After the last of the humans—including the news team—had left the riverside, the animals and birds quietly walked out from their hiding places. They all gathered beneath the avocado tree, where it was much cooler.

Stinger and his wasp thugs flew from across the river and perched on the trunk of the avocado pear tree.

Nanny Stush, Hebrew, and Jenny were the last ones to reach the group. Billy G looked around to see if all his colleagues were all right.

"Everybody okay, where are the visitors?" he asked.

The male Kling Kling blackbird hugged his girlfriend and looked at Billy G. "We are okay," he said. They had flown from their hiding place and perched beside Doc in the calabash tree.

"Am good too, Mr. Billy," said Doc.

Jacko looked around. "Everybody good, Billy G, especially White Squall." He laughed.

Billy G shook his head. "I certainly don't understand White Squall. Let him stay in the tree. I will have a talk with him later."

Nanny Stush looked toward the river. Is the crocodile still in the water?"

"Probably, but don't worry," said Billy G, "that was just a stunt to scare Lanky and Yabba. The croc is a friend of Stinger. He volunteered to help us. I just want to know if you are all okay."

Hebrew turned to Billy G. "So what would happen if the police never show up?"

"Nothing serious, my friend," said the old billy goat. "The croc was only going to bite at them up close. The objective was to let them experience the fear that Mongrel felt yesterday."

Hebrew nodded. "Okay, I understand."

Gramps, the one-legged rooster, turned to Hebrew. "Well, it work because Yabba pee-pee up himself, and Lanky Roy cry like a baby."

"A so the wicked behave when them back is against the wall," said Ras Blah Blah.

Hebrew lifted up her head toward the sky and closed her one good eye. "Well, thank you, Jesus, we couldn't do it without you. Lanky Roy is off to jail again."

"Yes," said Jacko, sitting on the ground. "Lanky Roy is quickly becoming Iron Bridge number one jailbird."

"Yes," said Jenny, jumping on Hebrew's back. "First, for thieving electricity, and now, animal cruelty and child abuse." From her position on Hebrew's back, she looked around at all her animal and bird friends. "Wait, where Grunty is?"

They all looked among themselves to see if the fat, oversized pig was among them, but Grunty was nowhere around.

"Grunty probly still running from the humans," said Jacko. "Probly knock down all a mi banana tree."

"Hey, guys, mi have news!" shouted a bird's voice from above. They all looked up and saw Kas Kas flying from the direction of the shortcut that led to the housing scheme. She landed in the middle of the group. "A have good news," she said.

"Really, Kas Kas, really?" said Lorna, who looked like she was close to having her puppies.

"Yes," said Kas Kas, nodding her head vigorously. "Peaches move out of the house."

Lorna looked at Kas Kas. "How we all know you telling the truth?"

"Well," said Kas Kas, "when the human news people come, a fly away to Lanky Roy yard to see what going on . . . ole habits die hard, a guess."

"You going die very hard if you don't stop carry wrong news on people," said Lorna.

"Is true she talking," said Putus, coming to Kas Kas's rescue. "A hear Clifton telling Mongrel that there will be no more Peaches to disturb them."

"Ohh, a see," said Jacko, "the news is correct this time, but it stale."

Billy G turned to Kas Kas. "Even if the news is stale, you're talking the truth, Kas. Very good, keep it up."

Kas Kas face beamed with pride as she absorbed the compliment from the president of the Animal Committee.

Jenny flew off Hebrew's back and landed on the ground beside Kas Kas. "Don't worry that the news is stale, Kas, at least you telling the truth. That is a start," she said, putting a wing around Kas Kas's shoulder.

"Wait, Jenny," said Jacko, looking at the female common fowl. "Shouldn't you be hugging somebody who have one leg?" he asked.

Gramps, the one-legged rooster, laughed. "Is the same thing a wondering too, Jacko."

"Oh please, Gramps," said Jenny, "your coupling days over."

They all laughed, including Jenny, who they haven't seen laugh in a very long time. They were all in a joyous mood. Even the wind was blowing against the tree branches, and the water in the river didn't seem to be moving lazily anymore.

"Okay, gentle peeps," said Billy G, turning to the rest of the crowd. "It's not celebrating time as yet.

"What do you mean?" asked Nanny Stush, taking a tiny step toward Billy G. "Our number one tormentor was just taken to jail, and his baby mother ran away." Most of the animals and birds supported Nanny Stush's comment with a nod of the head.

"Yeah," said Bucka T, turning to Billy G. "I personally don't think Lanky and Yabba will have the nerves to be cruel to another animal after them do time in jail for the offense."

"Yes, but remember Lanky Roy was acting on orders," said Billy G. "You notice he never mention Speng Shell's name to the police?"

There was a hushed silence among the large group of animals and birds. They all looked at one another. The wise billy goat had brought up a valid point.

Jacko walked up to Billy G. "Ehehm," he said, clearing his throat to break the thick silence. "Billy, a don't think Speng Shell going try anything now that Lanky Roy gone to jail."

Billy G tilted his head back to position the old eyeglass frame on his nose. "Take this from an old goat like me, Jacko, never get complacent. The committee isn't taking any chances. We all need to work on a strategy to bring down Speng Shell."

"I agree with you, Billy G!" shouted War Plane.

"But Speng Shell is a different kind of opponent," said one of the mongrel dogs from the Hungry Belly Crew. "A won't lie, a scare of him, the man have gun, not firecracker, gun."

A few of the animals, especially the dogs, supported the dog's point by nodding and looking at the billy goat.

"Listen, gentle peeps," said Billy G, looking at the worried crowd. "After today's courageous and successful mission, we should not be afraid of any humans or their guns. Furthermore, the hotter the battle, the sweeter the victory."

"A see you point," said Jacko.

"Conscious talk, Billy G," said Ras Blah Blah, the Rastafarian sheep. "We need to figure out a way to steal their bullets. A gun without bullets have no use, and most evil humans who own a gun are weak without that gun."

All the animals and birds agreed with Ras Blah Blah's suggestion. Billy G felt better because they were all seeing things from his point of view. "Good point, Ras," he said, turning toward the crowd. "We can take on any human, even the entire Jamaican Constabulary Force. We should never back down, let Jah rise, and his enemies be scattered!"

There was a huge deadpan silence. They all stared at Billy G. Some of their mouths were wide open. They couldn't believe that he had quoted a biblical phrase in the form of a Rasta talk.

Ras Blah Blah put a hoof in the air. "Real talk, Sir Billy!" he shouted. "I happy that the I realized, that with unity among all animals and birds—despite species or religion—we can overcome our adversaries. Something the human race failed to practice."

Hebrew nodded. She didn't care if the others saw her agreeing with the Rasta sheep. To her, the truth was the truth. "That is so true, Ras. I support you on that."

When all the other animals and birds saw that Hebrew publicly endorsed Ras Blah Blah, they all began to cheer with great enthusiasm.

"Yes, Ras, animal power!" shouted the Hungry Belly Crew.

The male Kling Kling blackbird smiled. "Christians and Rastas coming together to work as one. A love that."

"Yeah man, birds and animal unity!" shouted War Plane.

Out of the blue, No-Shame flew and landed beside War Plane. "Brothers-in-arms!" he shouted.

They all stopped and looked at the comical John Crow. No-Shame held up both of his wings in an apologetic gesture. "Sorry, people, a fall asleep on Lanky Roy clothesline. Is Clifton wake mi up and tell mi that it all over. Is pure big stone Clifton mother throw at mi when she see mi. So a come by the river to see if you all still here."

Billy G looked at No-Shame and shook his head. "You and White Squall, I don't know which one of you is worse as a lookout."

They all began to laugh at No-Shame; even the old billy goat joined in.

After they all had a fill of laughter, Billy G started to search the crowd with his eyes. "Where is Mouth-a-Massi?" he asked.

They all began to look among the crowd for the talkative parrot, but the public announcement bird was nowhere in sight.

"Where is Mouth-a-Massi, gentle peeps?" Billy G asked again. No one had an answer for the president of the Animal Committee.

Guana, the green lizard, who was on the lowest limb of the avocado tree, yawned. "No one doe see that mad bird since the meeting start, Billy."

"A need him to remind you all that a meeting will be keeping tomorrow night about the Speng Shell issue."

Gramps said, "Mouth Almighty gone AWOL on you, Billy G."

"Probly on one of him toilet break," said Bucka T, "or fall asleep after eating some weed seed."

"I'll put my life on the latter," said Billy G.

Jacko got up from the ground and began to stretch his upper legs. "Let mi tell you something, Billy," he said, "if it was Mouth-a-Massi Noah send out of the ark to find dry land, I can bet you, Mouth-a-Massi would return with a ganja branch in him mouth instead of a olive branch."

They all burst out in laughter. A few of them got up from their seated position and stretched their limbs.

Billy G saw that some of them were looking tired, so he decided to call it a day. "Okay, gentle peeps, that's it for now, go home and get some rest. See you tomorrow night at the meeting. Hopefully, we will find Mouth-a-Massi to announce the time."

Bruck Kitchen was the first one to walk away. He didn't want them to call on him to volunteer for anything. Billy G saw him leaving and called out to him. "Hey, Brucky, just a minute. A need to have a word with you."

Bruck Kitchen stopped and wondered what the old billy goat could want to talk with him about. He looked around at the rest of the animals and birds. They had all started to head home. He watched as Guana begged Hebrew a piggyback ride home. The friendly donkey agreed, and the green lizard leaped onto the donkey's back.

As Hebrew walked away with Guana and Jenny on her back, Jacko saw them and ran after them. "Hey, Guana," he said, "like how Hebrew coat gray, it probly easier to camouflage against than a white piece a paper."

"Look here, man," said Guana, "don't start the foolishness again. You hear mi?"

Billy G watched as Jacko continued to jive the green lizard. He looked at Bruck Kitchen, who was waiting for him. He flicked the old eyeglass frame off his nose with a hoof, and it fell to the ground. He purposely did that to stall for time. He wanted to make sure that it was only he and the cat left on the riverbank when he talked to him. He saw Ras Blah Blah a few yards downriver and changed his mind. "Ras, a want to talk to you too, just hang on for a minute," he said, taking up the eyeglass frame with his right hoof.

"No problem," said Ras Blah Blah. "The I is in no rush."

Billy G turned his attention back to Bruck Kitchen, who was waiting for him. He walked up to the thieving cat and stopped in front of him. "Thanks for waiting, Brucky, as I mentioned, I want to talk to you."

"What you want to talk to mi about now, Billy?"

"Well, Brucky," said Billy G, "don't think I never notice you sneaking out of the cave last night."

"A . . . a was tired, Billy, that's why a—"

"Oh come on, Brucky, you of all know that we have to stand up against these cruel humans," said Billy G. "A mean look what they did to your uncle Patah Puss."

"Uncle Patah run away from the community from when mi was a kitten."

"Really, who told you that, your mother?" asked Billy G.

"Not only she. Every animal in Iron Bridge know that—what you getting at, Billy G?"

"Brucky," said Billy G, looking to see if Ras Blah Blah was eavesdropping on their conversation. "Your uncle was killed by two male humans."

"Killed?" asked Bruck Kitchen.

"Yes, they hanged him with an electrical cord, put him in a crocus bag, and throw him in a gully," said Billy G. He looked at the cat who was shocked by the news of his uncle's tragedy. "I am sorry, Brucky. I never wanted to tell you, but after seeing you sneaking away last night, I figured telling you the truth would make you understand what we are trying to do."

Bruck Kitchen could not believe what he was hearing. "Electrical wire, crocus bag, and gully?" he said to himself. His mind flashed back to the evening before at the bottom of the gully. His four feet started to feel weary, so he sat on the ground. He couldn't believe that the old bones in the crocus bag in the gully were that of his uncle. The crocus bag and gully were too much of a coincidence, especially the electrical cord. He knew that it must have been because of his uncle's thieving ways why the two male humans killed him. A tear rolled down one of his eyes. He looked up at Billy G. "A need some time alone, Billy."

"Okay, I understand," said Billy G. "I have to talk to the Ras. Take it easy, if you need anything, just ask, that's what the committee is here for." Billy G walked away from the grieving cat and walked in the direction of the Rasta sheep that was waiting for him under the avocado tree.

Ras Blah Blah saw Billy G heading his way, and he walked to meet him. "Yeah, Billy G, you say you want to talk to the I."

"Yes, Ras, a really want to talk to you," said Billy G, adjusting the eyeglass frame on his nose. "Listen, um . . . I just want to say thanks for your valued suggestion this afternoon. You made some profound speeches a moment ago, and you seem to have some good leadership qualities to you. I can't deny that."

Ras Blah Blah laughed in his mind. He knew one day the old billy goat would thank him. He smiled and looked at the president of the Animal Committee. "Well, Billy, Jah said the stone that the builder refuse shall be the head cornerstone—"

"You don't have to rub it in, Ras." Billy G smiled. "Tomorrow night, I want to announce at the meeting that I want to vote for you as the vice president of the Animal Committee. Will you accept?"

Ras Blah Blah gave him a huge smile. "Yes, I will accept. Is all about unity. The I is looking forward to work with you, Billy. Let us work together to make the world a better place for all animals, birds, and insects." He held out a hoof toward Billy G. "One love," he said.

The wise old goat shook Ras Blah Blah's hoof and smiled. All hard feelings he had in his heart toward the Rasta sheep were gone. As the president of the Animal Committee, he felt he also needed to put his differences aside and work in unity with the Rasta sheep. "One love too, Ras. I agree with you. Teamwork is the key."

"Yeah, it good when leaders can come together as one and share ideas to make things better."

Billy G nodded. "Something the human race fails to practice, eh?"

"They fail every time, Sir Billy. The problem with the human race is their ego, but the Iron Bridge Animal Community won't fail because of ego."

"I totally agree with you on that," said Billy G. "I think you will make an excellent vice president—"

"Sir Billy," said a voice from behind them. They turned around to see a teary-eyed Bruck Kitchen standing behind them.

Billy G looked at Ras Blah Blah for a brief moment and then looked at the cat. "Yes, my friend, what can I do for you?"

"Um, what time the meeting going start tomorrow?" asked Bruck Kitchen.

Billy G looked at Ras Blah Blah again and smiled. "Well, I will let my soon-to-be vice president here decide on that."

Bruck Kitchen looked at the Rasta Sheep. "Congrats, Ras."

"Give thanks, Brucky," said Ras Blah Blah. "I would suggest we start the meeting in the early afternoon so it can over before it get dark. We don't want the birds and fowls to get lost in the darkness."

"That's a very good idea, Ras," said Billy G.

"Yeah, that make sense," said Bruck Kitchen, turning to Billy G. "A coming to the meeting tomorrow to give my suggestions."

Billy G smiled and nodded. He was pleased that Bruck Kitchen had finally come to his senses. "Very good decision, Brucky," he said. He held out his right hoof to Bruck Kitchen, and the cat shook the wise old goat's hoof with a paw.

Ras Blah Blah shook Bruck Kitchen's paw as well.

Billy G looked at Bruck Kitchen with a half-smile on his face. "Brucky, I'm dying to hear your suggestion at the meeting tomorrow evening."

"Me too," said Ras Blah Blah.

"You all want to hear it now?" asked Bruck Kitchen.

"Oh no, Brucky." Billy G laughed. "Keep it as a surprise. This is one suspense I definitely will enjoy."

They all laughed and walked off together downriver, discussing strategies for the next meeting as the warm afternoon sun shone on the Iron Bridge community below.